GW01035610

Ignatius
the Wonderful Pig

Patrick O'Sullivan

Blackwater Press

Also by the same author:
A Girl And A Dolphin

For the Chinese Year of the Pig,
a Token of Good Luck

© Copyright text: Patrick O'Sullivan

First published in 1995 by Blackwater Press, Unit 7/8, Broomhill Business Park, Tallaght, Dublin 24
Printed at the press of the publishers.

ISBN: 0 86121 815 9
British Library Cataloguing-in-Publication Data.
A catalogue record for this book is available farm the British Library.
O'Sullivan, Patrick. Ignatius The Wonderful Pig.

Editor: Deirdre Whelan

Cover Design/illustration: Aileen Caffrey

Contents

Chapter One

Lucy Connor was ten. She had china-blue eyes and wavy red hair falling loose about her shoulders. She lived in the small Kerry town of Ballymactaggle, a town dominated by the huge mass of the ancestral home of the MacTaggles, Ballymactaggle Hall. Hubert MacTaggle, the last of the old family, was now in his late seventies but he did not live alone at the hall. Here too, lived Kelly, the old man's butler, and Ignatius the wonderful pig.

It was one of the great unsolved mysteries of life as to how Hubert MacTaggle had first made the acquaintance of this extraordinary pig. One thing was certain, however, the butler was required to address the pig as "Master Ignatius" and special seating arrangements had to be made for him at the dining table.

Lucy's first encounter with Ignatius was one she would never forget. He came squealing towards her along the avenue like some half-demented creature with his tail on fire. Of course, she had seen him in the village, but there had never been a chance to get to know him. Now, here on the avenue, on a day of sunlight and shadow and faintly rustling leaves, she rubbed him and calmed him with her soft soothing words.

He had such wonderful eyes, warm and wise, his head tilted sideways like an attentive dog as if he were listening to everything she said. She sensed at once why Mr MacTaggle regarded him as a very special pig, but why was the pig so upset? She soon learned the answer, for the old man came dashing along the avenue in his shabby tweed suit, holding a bottle in one hand and a spoon in the other.

Lucy was tempted to beat a hasty retreat. Her friend, Rachel, insisted that MacTaggle was so daft he'd murder her and plant a gooseberry bush on top of her severed head at the bottom of the fruit garden.

"Ignatius! Ignatius!" gasped the grey-haired MacTaggle impatiently. "You know this cod-liver oil is good for you." Then he looked at Lucy and added. "Isn't it, my dear? Isn't it, my dear?"

There was such insistence in the old man's voice that she dared not contradict him, though if the truth were told she hated cod-liver oil.

"Now see, Ignatius, now see what a naughty boy you've been. This young lady will not say no to a spoon of cod-liver oil."

Lucy squirmed visibly before taking the spoon that was offered to her and gulped back the liquid as fast as he could – ugh! It tasted disgusting but she tried to pretend that she did not mind in the least. It was a few minutes before the pig was tempted to do likewise, after which he lifted his snout with aristocratic disgust. It was perfectly plain that he regarded cod-liver oil as something beneath his dignity. Poor old MacTaggle seemed very relieved, however, that the drama was over at last and invited Lucy back to the house. Rachel's words of warning still echoed inside her head but she chose to ignore them; if the cod-liver oil didn't kill her, nothing would.

The house was a massive house, built of old yellow stone in the 1840s, the different roof levels suggesting that there had been a number of additions down through the years. The pig, having made peace with his master and having regained his usual serenity, romped cheerfully before them, through the front hall. What MacTaggle's ancestors thought of a plump porker happily skipping through their stately home, Lucy could not guess. The faces in the portraits – fat, arrogant and without expression – remained as cold and aloof as the day they had been frozen in time by the artist's hand years and years before.

Ignatius came to rest on one of the large sofa chairs by the fire. MacTaggle summoned Kelly, the butler, who was also quite elderly and who seemed to waddle rather than to walk. They would have some tea and a few slices of angel cake – Master Ignatius' favourite – for Master Ignatius had a delicate tummy.

Lucy was spellbound by the many treasures in the drawing room – old clocks and paintings and ornaments and best of all, a grand piano. But MacTaggle wanted to hear all about herself and her friends and her family for he could see Master Ignatius was very taken with her and Master Ignatius was a very shrewd judge of character. Lucy told him that her father was a painter and decorator and her mother was a housewife who also worked part-time in the café in the summer.

And had she any bothers and sisters? Just one brother, Rory, two years younger than her, and she was always getting the blame when something went wrong, or was broken, even when Rory was the real culprit.

She would never forget her first visit to the drawing-room at the hall. Seeing is believing and she saw with her very own eyes a pig drinking tea from a china cup.

"China, of course – Master Ignatius regards anything else as a mug," explained MacTaggle seriously, handing a cup to Lucy. Lucy gaped in astonishment as the pig sipped his tea and sampled his angle cake with a delicacy that would have put many a human to shame. Next moment, however, her astonishment scaled new heights when the charming porker began to speak in the poshest accent she had ever heard!

" I simply cannot abide tea bags – so common, so vulgar," he insisted with the certainty of an expert. "One must have leaf tea or nothing, or one may as well be drinking dish water, don't you agree, my dear?" Lucy's hands trembled so visibly that the cup she was holding rattled in the saucer. Master Ignatius could speak! Master Ignatius could speak, his voice rich and cultured and self-assured. MacTaggle did not intervene; it was as if he regarded the pig's ability to talk as the most natural thing in the world.

"I don't really know much about tea," Lucy stammered at length. She could scarcely believe her ears, for now she was making conversation with a pig, a very extraordinary pig, but a pig nonetheless. There had been a time when the butler had had his doubts about his master's sanity for he heard the old gentleman chatting with the pig over dinner. But he too had since learned of Master Ignatius' secret.

"We had the most hideous tinned rice for tea last evening – lethal to one's digestion, of course," the pig continued. "Kelly, you see, had a sudden craving for rice and he would insist we all had a helping from the tin, there being nothing else to hand. So there, my dear, you have the reason why I've been obliged to swallow that ghastly cod-liver oil just now."

The more she heard of Master Ignatius, the more Lucy wondered about his ancestors. Had he come from a line of titled pigs? It seemed entirely possible. Might his grandfather have been Lord Precocious Pringle Pig and his grandmother Lady Priscilla Pernickety Pig? At any rate, it would not surprise Lucy in the least if Ignatius had royal blood in his veins. This was to be the first of many visits to the hall, even though at first her mother was a little anxious. Her father insisted, however, that the old man was a gentleman and the pampered pig was hardly likely to turn vicious.

Lucy went for drives with MacTaggle and Ignatius in the old man's old Ford motor car. A car which her father humourously described as being held together by rust. MacTaggle had an unusual approach to driving. When he came to the avenue gates he shot out onto the roadway without pausing to look right or left. The pig would be seated comfortably on the passenger's seat beside him with Lucy clenching her fingers in terror in the back seat.

"Do as I do, my dear – close your eyes," whispered Ignatius. It was not a suggestion which Lucy found even remotely tempting.

"Drivers! They call themselves drivers!" MacTaggle sometimes exclaimed in frustration as he tried to pass out this car or that, all of them usually much more modern than his own. Lucy's distress was not reduced by the fact that the driver had trouble with his eyesight.

"Is that a car or a van coming towards us, Ignatius?" he once asked his co-driver. His companion replied dryly:

"I rather fear it's a bus!"

Master Ignatius always wore a smart little necktie – the

ultimate in style amongst fashion-conscious pigs. Even when the car seemed ready to mount the ditch and plough wildly through the neighbourhood fields he remained entirely unruffled.

"I must say I really do prefer the tartan to the plain green – at least when the occasion is something less than formal," he observed one day, adjusting the necktie as he studied his reflection in the mirror. "The tartan makes just the right sort of statement – understated and casual – don't you agree, my dear?"

"Yes, Oh, yes," Lucy stammered, trying to disguise her terror as the car went careering towards a narrow bend. Next moment, out of nowhere, came a huge red lorry.

"Wow!" Lucy screamed in anguish as the lorry came speeding down upon them.

"So glad you approve, my dear. So reassuring when one's friends are on exactly the same wavelength as oneself," Ignatius observed, still smiling at his reflection in the mirror. Lucy held her breath as she waited to hear the metallic banging and clanging of metal but a moment later the lorry had grazed past the side of the car and she sighed with relief.

"These people and their little cars – they think they own the road!" was MacTaggle's verdict on what had just occurred. Lucy's nerves were still racing wildly.

The three of them never went to the village without paying a visit to Katie O'Shea or Katie the Baker, as she was known locally.

"And tell me, Mr Hubert, do Master Ignatius still be as partial as ever to my crusty loaves?" Katie asked in her grovelling way.

"Oh, most definitely, Katie," Mr Hubert answered, reassuringly. "Master Ignatius is most particular about his bread. Only the best will do!"

"Well isn't that a miracle, surely?" said Katie crossing herself in gratitude at having kept Master Ignatius' favour for so long. "For there's some in this parish do claim they're crippled with indigestion all on account of my grand crusty loaves." She strained over the counter and smiled down at the old man's companion. "But can't wan tell right off he's a pig of superior breeding, and when it do come to pigs I swear I could write a book on them,' she babbled, "whereas them others is as common as muck."

Master Ignatius held his head aloft, for though Katie was only a humble baker it had long been perfectly plain – to him at least – that she was a lady of some understanding. When Katie had wrapped one of the much prized loaves in orangey saffron-coloured paper, she scooped a few peppermint humbugs from a great glass sweet-jar on a shelf, put them into a brown envelope and handed them to Mr Hubert.

The pig was very fond of mint humbugs at any hour of the day or night, but especially as he lazed by the fire in the late evening and this was Katie's way of saying how much she valued his custom. There were times when in fanciful mood she dreamed of having a crest above her door and the crest would read *Katie O'Shea, Baker, By Appointment to His Excellency, Ignatius the Wonderful Pig!*

Of course Lucy also pottered about with the old man in the garden, much of which was hopelessly overgrown with weeds. She thought it strange that the pig was never even tempted to indulge in a little playful digging and rooting with his snout but then Master Ignatius was not your average pig.

"Rooting with one's snout, my dear?" he replied in blank amazement when she broached the subject with him one lazy afternoon under the pear tree. "That sort of thing is all very well for those doomed to become rashers but I hardly think it becoming for the more sophisticated pig: How should you like to go about all day long with your nostrils covered in mud?"

Lucy listened intently but she did not intervene.

"Cleanliness is next to godliness, they say, my dear, and I must say I find a little time on my exercise bike so much more rewarding than diversions of the farmyard variety."

Lucy smiled. She could just imagine Master Ignatius huffing and puffing on his exercise bike for twenty seconds or so and then pampering himself with a few mint humbugs or a slice of angel cake.

Of course, one or two of Lucy's school friends, especially Rachel Byrne, taunted her about her friendship with the old man. Lucy's mother had, however, warned her not to get involved in a disagreement with Rachel. Rachel's father owned the café where Lucy's mother worked during the summer. "Mad Mac," Rachel called the old Mr MacTaggle and she often wondered why he wouldn't see sense and send the swine to the bacon factory.

One afternoon, Rachel crept secretly into the coal shed, one of the many tumbledown outhouses that stood around the cobbled yard at the back of the Hall. When Master Ignatius appeared in the yard, Rachel began to whimper and the pig was attracted towards the coal shed at once. He had always regarded the coal shed with something approaching horror – so much grit and grime and dust – and all so harmful to one's lungs! This was why he insisted that Kelly the butler should wear a gas mask every time he went to fetch some coal for the old green Aga.

Now, however, the concerned pig put his fears aside, for there appeared to be someone in distress in the darkness within. Even in early summer the interior of the coal shed was black and gloomy and Master Ignatius stepped daintily about to avoid the grimy coals. The whimpering had stopped and he looked about him with deepening dismay.

A moment later, however, Rachel leapt from her hiding place and sprinkled him liberally from head to tail with a bag of coal dust. His eyes were blinded by the blizzard, the stillness reverberating with Rachel's delighted laughter. Master Ignatius began to take on the aspect of one of those strange black, pot-bellied pigs she had seen on television. Next moment she was bolting the door behind her, screaming "Sucker!" at the indignant pig, and racing away in glee. She grinned from ear to ear, more than pleased with the prank she had played on the pampered pig.

It was quite some time before MacTaggle and Lucy, who were busy in the greenhouse in the walled garden, heard the cries for help that came from the coal shed. The two of them went dashing down the garden pathway, old MacTaggle gasping for breath.

When at last the door of the coal shed was thrown open, Master Ignatius staggered out into the bright sunlight. Lucy and her companion gulped in amazement for Master Ignatius had all the appearance of a pig who had been rolling about in the coal.

"I have been the victim of a gross piece of trickery," he began in scornful, self-pitying tones and though Lucy felt sorry for him she could not resist a grin. Poor Ignatius! He regarded it as a minor disaster when he discovered a splash of mud on one of his trotters and now he might pass for a chimney sweep's apprentice.

Lucy suspected Rachel at once when she heard the story but she could not be sure. MacTaggle looked at Ignatius.

"I'm sorry, old fellow, but I'm afraid we must have you hosed down before you may take a proper bath," suggested old MacTaggle, directing Lucy to do the honours.

"Hosed down!" exclaimed Master Ignatius indignantly. "Muddy wellingtons, splattered leggings – those are the sort of things one hoses down – not one's person!" Then he paused to lift his eyes heavenwards in dismay. This was a new low and certainly not one he would choose to record in his diary, for like all well-bred pigs he kept a secret journal.

"It'll be fun," Lucy assured him as she turned on the hose, though it was plain at once that he was less than impressed with Lucy's notion of fun. Now he stood erect and scornful as the water flooded down about him – not only his skin but also his pride, soaked through and through, his tail dangling limp and droopy behind.

Some time later, however, Master Ignatius was soaking in a hot bath on the first floor. A small room had been remodelled as the pig's bathroom, much of the furniture having been stuffed into the already cluttered rooms nearby. An old Victorian bath took pride of place on a red oval rug in the centre of the room and Lucy was only too happy to fill the bath with warm water. She added sandalwood bath salts – Master Ignatius' favourite. Poor Ignatius was very relieved to be relaxing in the bath, sipping a glass of white wine. Meanwhile the butler stood nearby, ready to add a little more hot water to the bath when called upon to do so.

"Fetch me my plastic swan, will you, my dear?" Ignatius said to Lucy. "I feel quite unsettled in the bath without my plastic swan."

Lucy looked at him, and grinned. The average pig would have settled for a plastic duck but only a plastic swan was good enough for Master Ignatius.

Soon the aristocratic pig had placed his empty glass aside and was playing with his plastic swan which seemed to dip and dive in the frothy swell. All at once the pig began to hum to himself – a jaunty lilting little hum in a rather mellow tenor voice – and Lucy recognised the tune immediately as "The Kerry Dances". A pig, a swan, and the Kerry Dances – his new friend could do nothing but grin.

" 'Tis on the radio you should be, Master Ignatius – Radio Kerry's 'Rambling House' maybe!" suggested Kelly with genuine enthusiasm when Master Ignatius brought his song to an end.

"Thank you, Kelly. One is rather proud of one's voice, one must admit," observed the cool, cosmopolitan pig with a gracious smile. One of the basic rules of good behaviour was to know how to receive a compliment as well as give one, and he had made a serious study of the works on this subject. He had at any rate clearly forgotten the indignity of being hosed down; he was like that, quick to rise to indignation but equally quick to forgive and forget. This was just one of the reasons why Lucy liked him so much. Despite all his airs and graces, he was a big softy at heart and very loyal to his master.

An expression of that loyalty came the very next day when old MacTaggle yielded to an absurd fancy to make some jam of his own. As he put it, Master Ignatius was very partial to strawberry jam. Lucy was dragged into "Operation Jam" and had great fun helping to pick and prepare strawberries but the wise old butler shook his head in despair as he examined the fruit that bubbled in the great enamel pan on top of the old green aga cooker. The jam stubbornly refused to set and the end product was more suitable for drinking than eating.

Old MacTaggle was not in the least down-hearted, however, for he declared it "uncommonly fine jam", even when it slithered off his soda bread onto his shirt. Master Ignatius, too, gave the jam his seal of approval by lapping it delicately from the china plate, of course, that had been set before him on the table.

"I cannot quite see why so many diners must have their jam so lifeless and inert," he explained good-naturedly. " I much prefer mine with a little animation." Then he delicately wiped away the sticky trickles about his chin with his linen napkin, a napkin that was, of course, embroidered with his initials.

* * * * *

Ballymactaggle was blessed with a beautiful sandy beach and a secret pathway through the woods often took the man, the girl, and the pig onto the beach early in the morning in the summertime. Even though MacTaggle's train of thought tended to wander occasionally, Lucy was always fascinated by his stories, especially the stories of his childhood when he and his late brother had been taken down to the strand by their governess – a wizen-faced creature in black whom they had christened "the crow".

It was easy to see how much Master Ignatius enjoyed his stroll along the strand for it was one of the few places, if not the only place, where he seemed to cast all decorum and reserve aside. Lucy watched him closely when in the manner of an excited dog he rushed headlong towards the incoming waves, beating a hasty retreat whenever the crested waves came too close. Master Ignatius peered with some amusement at the seagulls as they dived intermittently into the rolling swell and then began to squabble amongst themselves.

Rachel's father, Tom Byrne, owned the café and the adjoining supermarket in the village. He also owned some donkeys which were hired out for rides along the sandy beach during the summer months. He paid one or two schoolboys a small weekly wage to take the donkeys to the beach each day and to hire them out to the visitors.

One fine summer's morning, Lucy and her companions came upon one of the boys, Gavin, rocking himself idly in a boat. He seemed to be lost in thought. Old MacTaggle wondered what was the matter.

"One of the donkeys, Jasmine, the old grey one, stumbled and fell and sprained her foreleg two days ago," Gavin explained with great earnestness. "Some idiot rode her on stony ground, so I took her up to the field straight away to give her a rest."

"Excellent idea!" observed MacTaggle approvingly, waiting to hear more.

"Then I went and told Mr Byrne, but he went mad. He said he wasn't going to waste his money on a vet when it was plain the donkey was finished," Gavin continued, sunlight glinting on his tousled auburn hair.

"I was in charge, he said, and I was responsible for what happened. He said I could take his rifle and shoot the donkey and put her out of her misery."

"Wicked!" exclaimed Master Ignatius without thinking and Gavin gaped at him. He tried to convince himself at once that the exclamation had come not from the pig but from his master.

"I couldn't bring myself to shoot poor Jasmine. It'd be like shooting a friend," Gavin persisted. "So I took her and hid her in a shack in your wood. I did my best to tend the sprain but now it's swollen and I don't know what to do. I told Mr Byrne that I shot her and he'll skin me alive if he finds out I lied to him."

Old MacTaggle placed his hand on the boy's shoulder reassuringly and told him not to worry. He would sort everything out but two days later Lucy's world was in turmoil. The old man died in his sleep and the Hall echoed with the sound of Master Ignatius' heartfelt sobs, his face flushed and his eyes swollen with tears.

"Such a noble old gentleman," sniffled the pig to Lucy as they sat beside the bed. Master Ignatius' tartan neckerchief had been replaced by another of sombre mourning black. A piece of black crepe was twined about his tail.

"Poor Hubert. Always felt so guilty when the wine wasn't chilled," the pig mused in downcast tones looking towards his master. "Always felt so disloyal when I had to make do with common digestive biscuits instead of my usual thin wafers."

Lucy did not interupt for it seemed to be relief to her friend just to have someone who would sit and listen to him.

"He was quite keen on my having gliding lessons, you know – a sort of birthday present," the pig continued. "The MacTaggles were always an aerial family and I felt such a cad having to decline his generous offer, for I declare I feel quite dizzy even at the top of the stairs." He paused and sniffled again, an elegant sniffle, of course. "All the MacTaggles took to the air," he said, "though he was too polite to mention that most of them came down to earth again, rather sooner than they planned."

He turned and looked seriously at Lucy. "That, my dear, will serve to explain some of the rather lopsided chimney stacks on the west wing."

Lucy tried hard to stifle a grin as she imagined some of the less than competent flyers having close encounters of the worst kind with the chimney stacks.

"It was said they had an early Christmas at the Hall one summer," Master Ignatius continued with the same gravity as before. "That was when Hubert's grand uncle came shooting down the chimney and gave a very fair impression of Father Christmas."

They were silent for a few moments before the pig whispered confidentially. "Of course, there were a few skeletons in the family cupboard."

Lucy looked at him curiously. She did not understand.

"Hubert's grand aunt Matilda, poor dear, laboured under the impression that she was a duck and never went out of doors unless

16

it was positively lashing with rain." It was with the greatest difficulty that Lucy remained serious. "Of course, Hubert had no head for figures – always consulted me on his investments portfolio – stocks and shares and that sort of thing, you know," the pig persisted. He looked towards the man in the bed again, evening sunlight slanting through the window. "Fiercely proud of his ancestry – you'll never believe what some dreadful scoundrel said one evening at dinner." Lucy looked at her companion intently and waited to hear more. "Accused Hubert of slurping his soup! 'None of the MacTaggles were soup-slurpers,' said Hubert, furiously rising from his place and banging his fist into his bread roll." Ignatius fell silent again.

"What happened then?" Lucy prompted in hushed tones.

"Oh, my dear, there would have been a duel," retorted the pig, "but as luck would have it, it started to rain."

Only Kelly and Lucy knew that Ignatius could speak and yet the mourners at the wake saw nothing unreasonable in shaking his foretrotter and offering him their condolences. After all, a pig must have feelings, too, especially a pig bred on white wine and wafer biscuits. Next morning the chapel bell, mournful and solemn, began to peal out across the grey drizzle. The funeral procession came to a halt. The coffin was removed and the villagers followed the principal mourners towards the grave which had been dug before a huge Celtic cross beside the back wall of the churchyard.

The minister read the prayers, his voice grave and intense, the sweeping rain seeking to add urgency to his words, the cawing of the rooks in the woods of the estate echoing faintly in the distance.

Lucy began to cry again. Not only was Ignatius' fate uncertain but old MacTaggle's efforts to improve the lot of the donkeys on the strand had come to an abrupt end. It was no great wonder then that Rachel's father turned away from the graveside with a smug smile of satisfaction on his flabby face. MacTaggle's nephew, a tall, slim-figured, lean-faced, young man would scarcely trouble himself with the welfare of a few local donkeys. That is if it were his intention to remain on at the Hall and he did not decide to sell the entire place, lock, stock and barrel.

Lucy could just picture Rachel's smirking grin if her family took possession of the Hall. Not only was her father a man of means, her mother was a woman of great pretensions and grand ideas. For now, however, Lucy had trouble enough with her own mother. She had decided to place their house on the market so that they could move in with Lucy's grandmother, who was not not feeling too well and who owned a fairly large house in County Cork.

It was as if Lucy's entire life had been tossed into a melting pot and no one could predict with any degree of certainty what the future might hold.

Chapter Two

When one of the MacTaggles died it had long been the practice for their nearest and dearest to treat some of the mourners to a drink in their favourite pub, the MacTaggle Arms. Kelly, acting on instructions from Master Ignatius, made it his business to see that the custom was now honoured once again.

"The little pigeen. He has a face like a Christian, God love him," said Bridge Hannafin, as she stood filling pints behind the counter. "And there was some used swear he could tell the time by counting the bongs of the grandfather clocks beyond at the Hall."

"Well, really!" Master Ignatius told himself resentfully, "as if one had to rely on the chimes to tell one the time of day. One's eyesight is not so defective that one cannot read the numerals at a discreet distance."

Lucy was there, too, and the pig seemed reassured by her presence. It takes one to know one, Rachel Byrne told herself pertly, as she smiled one of her saintly smiles. If a shining halo suddenly materialised above her head at that very moment it would not have seemed out of place. Her father, Tom Byrne, however, was in quarrelsome mood. For while all about him were singing the praises of Hubert MacTaggle, he did not feel in the least inclined to be generous.

"Will ye give over the lot of ye? He was as cracked as his grandmother's mug," he insisted. "Is any man sane that keeps a pig in the parlour?"

There were some who were tempted to express the view that Rachel's mother had never been accused of insanity, even though she had seen fit to enter into holy wedlock with a pig of a different kind.

"Oh, then, Mr Hubert was a good-natured soul," said Kelly in regretful tones, "for look at how he let the children bring the donkey to his field and how he sent for the vet to put her to rights."

"Ah, give me a break! You're almost as bad as him!" Tom, Rachel's father, retorted sourly. "He was nothing but a doting old fogey and now that he's out of the way, I'll make it my business to put my donkey – *my* donkey, do your hear – out of her misery."

"You'll do no such a thing, Tom Byrne," Kelly insisted grimly, "for I'll not be held responsible for what I'll do to the man who interferes with that dacent animal."

"She's my donkey, I say," Tom persisted with the same hostility as before, "and I'll not have the likes of you telling me what I can and can't do with her."

"She's not your donkey, for you never looked after her right and proper," Kelly countered strongly.

Master Ignatius' eyes shone with defiance, too, and he was proud, so proud of Kelly, his master's good and faithful servant. "Apart from her leg being sprained, wasn't there bare patches on her back and her hooves hadn't been clipped since God knows when!"

"And his lordship made a right song-and-dance about it, too," Tom retaliated. "Telling me I wasn't fit to own a duck, let alone a donkey, but I put him in his place, so I did, for we can't all have pigs and donkeys at the table with us, says I. Some of us must go out to earn a crust."

"Well, you'll not put me in my place," Kelly insisted, "and that donkey is staying put."

"We'll see what the old man's nephew has to say about that!" Tom replied ominously, for the newcomer had not condescended to join the mourners in the pub – a decision which Bridge Hannafin took as a personal slight to herself and her pub.

"Any man as don't care to drown his sorrows with a pint after a good and pleasant funeral don't be no class at all," she whispered confidentially to Kelly. "And I'll not tell a lie, but he do have shifty eyes and shifty eyes was ever a bad sign."

Over the next few days Lucy and Gavin visited Jasmine, the donkey that the old man had kindly allowed to graze on his lands, having summoned a vet to tend to her injuries.

Old MacTaggle had talked of donating a field or two towards the establishment of a Friends of the Donkey Society, where old and unwanted donkeys could spend the last years of their lives. It had become something of a passion with the owner of the Hall ever since he had seen the wretched condition of poor Jasmine. She was already beginning to look much better, however. The hair on her back had begun to grow again and she did not seem to be nearly as lame as she had been a few weeks before.

There was a smile of joy in Gavin's deep, brown eyes, as he watched the little donkey graze contentedly about the base of a giant oak tree that grew in the centre of the field.

"What did your mother say when she heard you lost your job with the donkeys?" Lucy asked.

"She didn't mind," Gavin answered, with a shrug of his shoulders. He paused and grinned. "MacTaggle really told Tom off when he came to claim back his donkey, didn't he?"

"Jasmine was like a damsel in distress and MacTaggle was her knight in shining armour," Lucy mused in fanciful mood.

"Well, she'd better beware for her brave knight is dead and the fire-breathing dragon, Tom, is still on the warpath," Gavin replied ominously.

"I wonder how Ignatius is getting on," Lucy resumed abruptly. She had heard that MacTaggle's will was being read in the village that very morning and she was hoping Gavin would suggest they might seize the chance and visit the Hall. He did not do so, and so she had to made the suggestion herself.

It was a notion which didn't appeal to Gavin but a few moments later he and Lucy were crouching behind a cluster of laurel bushes – speckled and glossy – that grew on the right-hand side of the avenue. Lucy assured her friend that Kelly wouldn't leave the Hall and the coast would be clear as soon as MacTaggle's nephew passed by in his car.

The seconds seemed to drag by like hours and Gavin was beginning to wonder how he had ever allowed Lucy to talk him into such an escapade. What if MacTaggle's nephew had a wife?

What if she stayed behind at the Hall while her husband went to the village?

Seconds later, however, the huge white car went whizzing by, the hard lean face of the driver just a blur before their eyes. Soon they crept like foxes from their hiding place and hurried along the avenue, the woodlands on either side soon giving way to untidy lawns, shrubberies and ragged box trees. The great house itself, with its walls of sombre yellow stone and shuttered windows, seemed strangely cold and unwelcoming.

Lucy hesitated, her heart throbbing. Would they run round to the back of the house? Kelly spent a great deal of time in the old Servants' Hall near the kitchen. Or would they press the front doorbell? On impulse the girl pressed the bell; the gaping jaws of the gargoyled faces about the windows seemed repulsive as the buzz of the bell reverberated through the stillness within.

"Come in! Come in!" the grey-haired Kelly insisted in urgent tones after shuffling towards the door.

He was a stocky man and though his skin was lined and his eyesight fading, his was a face that was strong and dignified. He hurried as best he could before them along the front hall, leading them through dark and gloomy corridors that seemed to extend endlessly before them.

"The new man, Mr Hubert's nephew, he's a holy terror!" Kelly explained with the same urgency as before. 'Take that repulsive porker to the market,' says he to me. 'And sell him to the highest bidder.'" He paused to catch his breath. " 'Beggin' your pardon mightily, sir,' says I to him, 'but there's them will think I'm losing my senses if I do take the pig to a cattle mart.'"

Lucy giggled, but Gavin was somewhat over-awed by the stillness and gloom of the corridors. " 'And,' says I, 'Mr Hubert was mightily attached to Master Ignatius and 'twill be a great surprise to me if he's not after making some arrangements for him in his will.'"

"Oh, wouldn't it be brilliant if he did?" Lucy intervened with enthusiasm.

"'All right,' says his lordship, 'we'll wait till the readin' of the will,'" Kelly went on as they drew near to the door of the old Servants' Hall, " 'but in the meantime,' says he, 'I want that porker shifted out of the house and lodged in one of the kennels out the back.'"

"Poor Ignatius," Lucy thought. "Not only had he lost a master who doted on him, he had also to endure the indignity of being transferred to a kennel."

"However, I do bring him to the Servant's Hall every time Mr Peregrine clears off out of our sight."

The old man turned the door knob and the children found themselves in a cluttered room. The lower half of the walls were covered in mahogany, the upper half painted in faded blue and weighed down with prints of very kind, mainly of hunting scenes and ships. There were chairs and armchairs, a trunk, a writing desk, a little table, a bookcase, pots of geraniums, shelves laden with bric-a-brac. Lucy ran towards Ignatius who languished in a chair beside the grate, colourful tiles, years old, about the mantle, and an old gramophone with a magnificent horn in the background. She took one of the pig's foretrotters tenderly in her hand and smiled at him reassuringly. Poor Ignatius. He looked so dejected.

"A repulsive creature! Is one come to this at last?" he asked, sipping now and then from the glass of white wine that stood on a side table. "Peregrine, I may say, is the most ignorant creature that has ever set foot in this hallowed establishment. I heard him laughing heartily in the yard this morning, strutting about like a peacock and pleased as punch that dear Hubert is dead."

"But did he come to visit when Hubert was alive and did they like each other?" Lucy probed. Gavin now knew of Ignatius' secret too and Kelly listened intently.

"Oh, he made an appearance once in a blue moon, my dear," Ignatius explained. "He wasn't here a day when they were at each others throats. But you see he was family, and family was the most important thing in the world to Hubert – though Peregrine had the most dreadful habits."

"What habits?" Gavin probed.

"He smoked the most hideous cigars after dinner and deliberately blew the smoke into one's eyes," Master Ignatius retorted with a sigh. "So childish, so uncouth – no amount of mint humbugs could mask that awful aroma – the geraniums positively wilted." Ignatius paused and fumbled with the glass in his hand.

"And he had the cheek to refer to me as 'Old Rasher Head' when Mr Hubert was not about. One was never a vicious pig but one was quite tempted at times to drain the contents of the sauce-boat into his pockets – and now you have the reason for his hatred towards me."

Lucy grinned. She could just imagine Peregrine dipping his hands into pocketfuls of sauce.

"Quite the most dreadful billiards player one has ever encountered – wielded the cue with all the style of a woodsman with an axe."

It was then that Kelly suggested that Gavin should play the melodeon. Lucy and Ignatius were more than a little reluctant to accept the suggestion but some moments later he and Lucy were waltzing about in the limited space they had made for themselves in the centre of the room, the pig having expressed a preference for a waltz rather than a jig.

"We often had dance evenings after Mr Hubert's dinner parties," he explained, his movements graceful and elegant. "One quite charmed the company with one's little waltz and though some of the ladies made a practice of treading on one's toes, one was quite the favourite. One's dance card would be full before a note was played and from the disappointed ones it would be nothing but 'Master Ignatius, I do think it bad of you that you could not see fit to fit me in this time.' All one could do in the circumstances was bow graciously and say, 'Perhaps another time, dear ladies, perhaps another time.' "

Lucy grinned again. The very notion of ladies of fashion clamouring for a dance with a pig filled her with glee.

"And what did you wear?" she asked with interest, for she

could see how much Master Ignatius enjoyed thinking about the old days.

"Oh, one's bow-tie and tails, of course, my dear," Ignatius replied. "One felt positively naked without one's tails in those days."

When the music and dancing came to an end, Gavin helped Kelly to make some tea in the nearby pantry. Lucy seized the opportunity to have a few private words with her friend.

"The most depressing part of all, my dear, is that that upstart, Peregrine, is planning to stay on at the Hall," the pig resumed. "He asked Kelly if he knew of a painter and decorator who could carry out the necessary redecoration – work for your father, if he wanted it."

"My dad could do with the work," Lucy admitted. "Things have been a bit slack this past while, but are you sure you wouldn't mind, Ignatius?"

"Oh, it makes no difference to me," Ignatius assured her, his blue eyes a little brighter now. "If your father doesn't do the job, someone else will." He paused and looked at his companion with still greater intensity. "But tell me, my dear, how is Jasmine doing?"

"Oh, she's fine, but she can't stay here forever. Peregrine will want her off his land and where will she go then?" Lucy asked. It was a question that seemed to rouse the pig from his lethargy.

"Hubert had a dream of giving some land for the setting up of a donkey shelter," he reminded his companion. "Some will say it was a foolish dream, the dream of a silly old man, but you and I and Gavin and Kelly, the four of us together, we must do our best to make the dream come true!"

"Oh, yes, I'd love to help," Lucy agreed, "but what can we do?"

"We must hold our fire until we find out the terms of the will and until we are quite sure of 'the horrid one's' intentions," Ignatius answered.

"The horrid one," Lucy repeated with a grin. Lucy and Gavin enjoyed their tea with the butler and Ignatius but they did not wish to outstay their welcome. They were fearful lest the new master of the Hall might return sooner than expected.

"Goodbye, my dear," Ignatius said to Lucy, "and next time you call don't be surprised if you find me barking and burying bones. One has developed something of an identity crisis being confined to that awful kennel."

When Lucy returned to the little terraced house in the village, she found her mother busily cleaning the kitchen cupboards. Ever since the house had been advertised for sale, her mother had taken it upon herself to make an unrelenting assault on every speck of dust that came to her attention.

"I want you to tidy your room, Lucy. There are some people coming tomorrow to look at the house,' she said with great enthusiasm.

"I don't see why we have to sell our house at all," Lucy retorted with a groan, as she sat at the kitchen table. "After all, all our friends are here and Granny doesn't want anyone moving in with her. I heard her tell you so on the phone."

"Ah Lucy, it isn't as if we're emigrating to outer Mongolia – if we do move, we're only going to County Cork," her mother insisted.

"Dad feels the same way as I do," Lucy went on. "He says we'll be living in the back of beyond."

"Oh he does, does he? And I suppose he thinks Ballymactaggle is the centre of the universe," her mother retorted as she unscrewed the cover from a jar of cranberry sauce and sniffed the contents. She had bought it for the Christmas dinner the year before but neither her darling husband nor her darling children had condescended to eat any of it.

"You won't know yourself if we move in with Granny – such big rooms," her mother went on with the same enthusiasm as before.

"I think we've room enough in this house," Lucy said stubbornly.

"Will you look around you child? Will you look at the size of the kitchen? Some people have bigger cardboard boxes." She replaced the cover on the jar of cranberry sauce and returned it to the back of the cupboard. "And if the people come tomorrow while I'm down at the café, I want you to be nice and polite to them and show them around."

Lucy arched her eyebrows – she hoped against hope that the notion of selling the house was just another of her mother's crazy fads and that they would not go through with it if someone did eventually offer to buy it. Where was her father anyway? Down in the village painting one of the bedrooms above the café, her mother told her.

"If it's Rachel's bedroom, I hope he makes a right mess of it," Lucy said.

"Ah, why can't you try and get along with Rachel?" her mother sighed. "She's impossible – that's why. She had no right to call Mr MacTaggle 'Mad Mac', and worse still to call me 'the pig lover'."

"She meant nothing by that. Sure didn't the world and his mother know he was odd, the poor man, for who in their right mind keeps a pig in the parlour?"

"Some people keep dogs and cats in their parlours," Lucy argued. "Budgies and canaries and goldfish, too – so what's so awful about being kind to a pig?"

"So that's what's eatin' you! You're worried about the pig!" her mother replied, abandoning her place at the cupboard and moving towards the table. "He'll be fine, never fear, and I didn't mean anything bad about poor MacTaggle when I said he was a bit odd. He was the finest gentleman in the county in his day. Got on well with the people around him by all accounts."

Lucy fidgeted with a mug on the table. She couldn't help worrying about Ignatius. He was her friend, and people worried about their friends. "Of course, they do," her mother agreed, "but work is the best thing to take a person's mind off their problems. So why don't you tidy your room like I say, and we'll have a nice bit of dinner later on."

Lucy roused herself and went upstairs where she immediately set to work tidying her wardrobe. The shelf above the rail of clothes was cluttered with magazines, dolls, jigsaws, colouring books and small computer games. It would take her ages to arrange them in some kind of order.

She glanced at the bed with its pretty primrose quilt – the notion that someone other than herself might be sleeping in her bed in a few weeks time did not appeal to her in the least. Soon she heard the doorbell chime downstairs followed by the unwelcome sound of Rachel's voice. She hoped her mother would say she was out somewhere, but seconds later Rachel was climbing the stairs and was soon standing in the doorway of the bedroom.

She would love to give Lucy a hand, but she was whacked out from all the washing-up at the café. Lucy rolled her eyes. What a fibber! Rachel never washed a cup in her life! Rachel sat on the bed and flicked idly through the pages of a magazine. She produced a packet of cigarettes, placed one in her mouth and lit it!

"I'm not offering you one, Lucy, because you being a goody-goody, you'd only say no," she said glancing casually at the magazine once more.

"Put it out! If my mother sees you smoking in here she'll have my life," Lucy insisted, and hurried to turn the key in the door.

Rachel took another drag of the cigarette and exhaled the smoke through her mouth.

"I suppose you think it's cool to smoke?" Lucy said.

"Yeah, as a matter of fact, I do," Rachel retorted pertly. "Beats hangin' around with some mad man and a pig."

"MacTaggle wasn't mad and Ignatius isn't just a plain ordinary pig," her companion countered. She had thought she would get some bit of peace while her brother was away in the Gaeltacht but trust Rachel to come round and stick her oar in where it wasn't wanted.

"Oh, sorry, Lucy luv, I forget you're a pig luvver," Rachel

grinned sarcastically, "but I'm a little more choosy about the company I keep." She closed the magazine and blew rings of smoke from her mouth. "My dad says he's going to buy the pig from Peregrine MacTaggle," she went on in provocative tones, "and he's planning to have a big bash at the café. You're invited, of course. I know you'll like the roast pork and apple sauce."

Lucy fumed with rage.

"Rachel Byrne, you're nothing but an old troublemaker," she said vehemently. "I'd rather eat a bit of my own leg than eat Ignatius – and besides, Ignatius is very popular in the village. An awful lot of people wouldn't take it too kindly if anything happened to him."

"Not much they can do to help him though, is there, when my father gets a carving knife and sticks it through his belly?" Rachel smirked.

Lucy was about to launch forth on another attack when there came a knock at the door. It was Lucy's mother. Rachel leapt from the bed and flung the lighted cigarette out of the window. Lucy's mother wondered for a moment about the locked door but it was only a fleeting thought.

She had just had the strangest telephone call, she explained with bewilderment. Mr Philbin, the solicitor, had telephoned to say that MacTaggle had mentioned Lucy in his will.

"Fancy that, Lucy. Mentioning you in his will?" her mother mused in the same bewildered tones.

"Did the solicitor tell you anything more?" Lucy asked, her bright blue eyes gleaming with surprise.

"Yes, oh, yes," her mother replied. "It seems that MacTaggle has appointed you as legal guardian of the pig and the pig will be delivered some time later today."

"What? Are you sure?" Lucy exclaimed, jumping for joy. "You mean Ignatius is coming to live with us here?"

"Seems like it," her mother retorted with less enthusiasm than before.

"Do you hear that Rachel Byrne?" Lucy crowed triumphantly.

"Your father will have to find himself another pig and if he asks who gave you the message, tell him you heard it from Master Ignatius' legal guardian."

Rachel was suitably annoyed. The telephone call from the solicitor had clearly spoiled her fun. She suddenly said that she had to be getting back to the café or her mother would be wondering where she was.

Lucy threw her arms about her mother.

"Ignatius coming to live with us – what luck!"

"What luck?" her mother repeated with more than a hint of uncertainty.

Chapter Three

Later that day, Kelly, the butler, acting on the instructions of Mr Philbin, the solicitor, delivered the pig to the terraced home of the O'Briens. He was mightily relieved – mightily relieved that Ignatius had found a good home, for who could predict what might have befallen him if he had to spend another few days at the Hall. Naturally, the kindly butler had packed a few of Master Ignatius' favourite things in a suitcase.

Lucy was overjoyed as she led Ignatius into the living-room and asked him to take a chair by the fire. The small, pink living-room wasn't nearly as grand as the plum-coloured drawing-room at the Hall but she was sure Master Ignatius would be very happy with them. Lucy's mother could scarcely believe her eyes. What would the neighbours say if they saw a pig sitting sedately in one of her best armchairs, an armchair that had cost her an arm and a leg at a fancy furniture shop in Tralee.

"And there's more good news," the grey-haired butler assured the woman of the house.

"More good news?" Lucy's mother repeated quizzically, a tremor of fear in her voice.

"Yes, Philbin will be telling ye the full story," the butler enthused, "but Mr Hubert is after seein' to it that Master Ignatius will have a monthly income for as long as he lives – just enough for his upkeep and so forth."

Lucy's mother looked at Master Ignatius. A pig with a monthly income! It was becoming more and more bizarre. On the other hand, she had known one or two human pigs in her time and they had not been mocked for having a monthly income.

"And what about the land for the donkeys? Was there anything about that in the will?" Lucy asked anxiously.

"Well you might ask," Kelly grinned, "for didn't Mr Hubert only go and leave two fine fields to Master Ignatius to do with as he playses. As Master Ignatius' guardian 'twill be your job to ensure that any plans Master Ignatius might have for the land are acted upon."

It was at this point that Master Ignatius couldn't resist leaping up from his place. He turned to Lucy's mother and said, "This calls for a celebration, my dears, we must have white wine and strawberries and angel cake at once."

"Bless us and save us, Lucy, is the pig after speaking to me? Such a fancy twang as he has," exclaimed her mother, going weak at the knees. "But sure where would we be getting white wine? The bottle I got last Christmas was here for months and months and not a one of ye'd look at it for me, till the day your father used it for stripping the paint off the back of the kitchen door, that is."

"Don't be alarmed, dear lady," replied Ignatius in his reassuring way, moving towards her and taking her by the hand. "Now that I have means at my disposal, I think we may hope for something better than turpentine."

"Oh, to be sure, Master Ignatius, to be sure, and can't we send out for whatever it is takes your fancy when I recover my senses – in an hour or two!" said Lucy's mother, still trembling at the knees.

"Oh, wouldn't it be great if we could do something to help the old unwanted donkeys?" Lucy said in excitement, "then MacTaggle's dream would come true."

"There was some did say Hubert MacTaggle was after losin' his marbles entirely," the butler resumed in a pensive mood. "And to tell ye the truth, I was put to the pin of my collar at times when I couldn't make head nor tail of what he was trying to say." He paused a moment to savour another draught of brandy from the glass. "But he did have a great *ghrá* for the animals and any man do have a way with the animals do have his heart in the right place, I say." He paused again and smiled at the pig. "Yourself and Master Ignatius will have to draw up a plan of action and ye can count on me to give ye every support."

These expressions of goodwill were rudely interrupted when

there came a loud knock at the front door. Who should come amongst them but an irate Peregrine MacTaggle.

Peregrine was in his late twenties. Tall and lean and dark haired, his expression was unmistakably hostile.

"I'm not having a pig deny me what is rightfully mine," he asserted in a determined voice, a dark blue handkerchief peeping through the breast pocket of his finely tailored jacket. "This monthly income is ridiculous enough, but I just cannot accept the loss of two of the biggest and finest fields on the estate." He glanced at the pig in the armchair.

"I'm a reasonable man, I won't object to the monthly income if Master Ignatius" – there was a biting sarcasm in his tone – "if Master Ignatius surrenders his claim to the fields."

"Steady on, sir," said the butler rising weakly from his place. "Do you want Master Ignatius to fly in the face of Mr Hubert's generosity?"

"Mr Hubert was a senile old man," the newcomer insisted. "He was hard pressed to remember his own name at times, and his obsession with this pampered papoose was a clear sign of his less than stable state of mind."

Lucy looked towards Master Ignatius. She could see that he was seething with rage at the reference to Hubert as a senile old man. But Peregrine was unaware of his secret and he didn't want to betray himself now.

"He left you the rest of the estate," Kelly countered. "Was he doting then, too?"

"You didn't do too badly yourself, Mr Kelly," the uninvited guest retorted with a smirk. "If you are ever forced to leave your post at the Hall I shall not only have to provide you with alternative accommodation but also to pay your wages."

"Mr Hubert was a kind old gentleman and no mistake," the butler replied, placing his glass on the mantlepiece, "and 'twouldn't be fittin' if his wishes weren't carried out to the letter of the law."

"Since the matter of the two fields does not concern you, I

33

would appreciate it if you did not get involved," Peregrine retorted haughtily. He turned to Mrs O'Brien who had remained silent in the background. She looked more confused than ever. This was turning out to be one of those days when she wished she had stayed in bed in the morning. But wasn't it the will of God that she had given the living-room a good going over, for it would be criminal if Mr Peregrine made fun of her amongst his posh friends.

"According to the terms of my granduncle's will, your daughter is now the pig's legal guardian," he told Lucy's mother in a tone that still betrayed his utter sense of disbelief. "If she agrees to surrender the fields to me I might consider coming to some settlement with her."

"B..but?" Mrs O'Brien stammered.

"But?" Peregrine prompted.

"But how can my daughter come to a settlement when she don't even own the fields, for as you said yourself, 'tis the pig owns the fields."

Mr Peregrine sighed. He was beginning to wonder if he hadn't made a dreadful mistake when he'd decided to spend the rest of his life in this god-forsaken country. "You can hardly expect me to enter into negotiations about property matters with a pig!"

"Mrs O'Brien don't expect you to do anything, sir, except maybe to keep a civil tongue in your head when you're talking to her in her own house," Kelly intervened again.

Mr Peregrine removed his handkerchief and dabbed his forehead. He might as well be speaking Swahili for all the impact his words were having on those about him. Finally he turned his attention to Lucy who stood beside Ignatius' armchair.

"Lucy," he began in softer tones, "I want to be straight with you. I propose to try and make a go of the estate. That's a big job even with all the land, but without those two fields it's next or nigh impossible." Lucy listened intently, her bright blue eyes, keen and perceptive. "What would you do with those fields anyway? Think about that," Peregrine asked.

"Master Ignatius wants to set up a place for stray and unwanted donkeys," Lucy replied honestly. Mr Peregrine was becoming more and more frustrated, but he tried not to show it.

"Mr MacTaggle was fond of animals that had been cast aside. He said he knew what it was like to be alone in the world, unwanted and unloved," Lucy explained.

"I'm sure that's a very nice idea, Lucy," the newcomer replied with a smile, "but a bit impractical. You'd need a shelter for the donkeys for one thing. You just couldn't let them freeze outdoors in the winter. Have you thought of how much a building like that would cost?" Lucy shook her head. "Add to that the cost of fodder and feedstuffs. If some of the donkeys were old and unwell, you would have to build up their strength, and all the donkeys would need extra feeding in the wintertime when there would be little or no grass."

"I don't think Lucy's given the idea of helping the donkeys much serious thought," Mrs O'Brien intervened, but it was an intervention which displeased her other two guests – Ignatius and Kelly.

"And you would have to have someone to keep an eye on the donkeys when you were at school," Peregrine resumed with some enthusiasm for at last there seemed to be a glimmer of hope that he might be winning the argument. "Someone to clean out the shelter and put down new bedding when that was needed – and don't forget there would probably be a lot of veterinary bills, too. It would make a lot more sense to allow the fields to remain part of the estate and in return for this concession I would pay you a sum of money to be agreed between us."

Lucy hadn't thought too deeply about the problems that might surround the foundation of the shelter and Mr Peregrine's argument seemed reasonable and convincing. However, she felt she would not be living up to MacTaggle's trust in her if she did not make some effort to make his dream a reality.

"Master Ignatius has the final decision," Lucy explained to the self-assured young man before her.

"Oh, of course, of course," he retorted in the tone of one attempting to cajole an obstinate infant to see sense, but Lucy hadn't finished.

" Master Ignatius wants to press ahead with the shelter for the donkeys," she asserted, a triumphant gleam appearing in the pig's bright eyes.

Mr Peregrine sighed and moved towards the door. He had come with the intention of making these people see sense but obviously they could not see sense if it bit them on the big toe. He had, however, one last line of attack. There was a great deal of renovation work – painting and decorating – to be done at the Hall which his grand uncle had allowed to fall into a state of disrepair.

Mr O'Brien had been recommended to him as an excellent painter and decorator and he would be more than happy to employ him if these foolish notions about a shelter for donkeys were cast aside. Mrs O'Brien did not know what to say when she showed the elegant Mr Peregrine to the door, but she tried hard to be polite by assuring him that her daughter would carefully consider what he'd said.

"Conceited fool!" Master Ignatius said indignantly when Peregrine had gone. "How gracious of him not to object to my monthly income if I surrender my claim to the fields." Hereupon the aristocratic pig rose from his place and held his head aloft, his shoulders erect and proud as if standing to attention. "No surrender, say I, no surrender. You and I, my dear – we will fight the good fight and lead our troops to victory!"

A few strains of the national anthem would not have gone amiss at that very moment and Lucy could not resist a grin. Ignatius became so passionate at times and she fancied him now imagining himself at the head of a death-defying charge against enemy lines, shooting mint humbugs and strawberries at the craven-helmeted figure of Peregrine whose head strained above the trenches only now and then.

When Lucy's father came home from work that evening he was

given a detailed account of every thing that had happened by his still excited wife. Lucy's father was a plain, quiet, sensible man who was strongly of the view that communication was always better than confrontation.

The offer of work at the Hall was very tempting but Lucy, who was now taking Ignatius for a stroll, must make up her own mind when it came to a decision about the fields. People had been very quick to insist that old MacTaggle was stone mad but he himself had more respect for a man who was kind to animals than the likes of Tom Byrne who made a tidy sum out of the donkeys on the beach and who never troubled himself to see the donkeys were in good health.

Mrs O'Brien didn't know what to think – the house up for sale, a pig sitting in the front room all afternoon long, and her daughter his legal guardian. And Lucy wanted the pig to spend the night in her bedroom! He was perfectly clean, fully house-trained, and he would do no harm at all lying on the mat beside the bed.

That was carrying things too far when they had a perfectly good shed at the bottom of the back garden. Lucy's father, however, had a soft spot for Ignatius. He had seen him round the village several times and had always thought of him as a refined, well-mannered pig. He had got to know him even better about two years before when old MacTaggle had had a sudden notion that he wanted all the window frames and shutters repainted. This was the only improvement he had made at the Hall in years – and Lucy's father had been given the job. He'd seen how Master Ignatius had enjoyed the freedom of the whole house and how well behaved he had been. They should allow Lucy to have her way for the time being and in the unlikely event of Ignatius not living up to expectations he could be "deported" to the shed at the bottom of the garden.

Master Ignatius, however, was something less than content with the mat and so made himself comfortable on the bed cover at the foot of Lucy's bed where he curled up like a great pink cat.

"Do you snore, my dear?" he asked abruptly, the note of

concern in his tone clearly audible.

"No, no, at least I don't think so," Lucy retorted hesitantly.

"That is a relief!" the pig insisted with a sigh. "One of Hubert's little failings, I fear, and one that led to many a sleepless hour on my part, though one was obviously too tactful to broach such a delicate matter with one so kind."

"Did old MacTaggle snore?" Lucy inquired.

"Oh, yes. The MacTaggles were all snorers. Quite a family tradition," Ignatius explained. "There never was a MacTaggle who didn't snore but listening to another's snores can be so tiresome when one is wide awake at three in the morning, don't you find?"

"Yes, yes," Lucy replied in agreement, grinning at the notion of a pig who took exception to snoring.

"And Peregrine was quite the worst of the lot," Ignatius persisted. "Such resonant snoring that one was quite concerned for the safety of the tilting chimney stacks. One's last resort was a pair of woollen ear muffs – a present from Aunt Euphemia. Though one has always regarded the wearing of ear muffs – especially in bed – as something less than tasteful." Another silence followed, Lucy repressing a giggle.

"I'm so glad you've come to stay, Ignatius," she resumed with a warmth that could not be mistaken.

"And so am I, not only glad but also relieved," replied the pig. "I was beginning to wake up in the mornings and always the same question was in my head. 'Am I a pig or am I a dog?' That's what comes of being incarcerated in a kennel and one didn't even have the reassurance of a mirror."

"Well, there's no need to ask yourself that question any more," mused Lucy, lying contentedly on the flat of her back. "Everyone knows you're the swankiest pig in Kerry."

"Too kind, my dear, too kind," Ignatius replied in his gracious way.

"And if you have trouble falling asleep I'll read you a story. I've lots of stories and Rory never lets me read to him," Lucy assured him.

"Oh! Excellent! Excellent!" said Master Ignatius, "Hubert sometimes read to me, too, but the poor dear usually fell asleep halfway through."

"I'd like to be your friend like MacTaggle was," Lucy concluded with an earnestness that impressed her companion.

"You already are my dear, You already are," the pig told her with conviction. Soon, very soon, she and her new companion were fast asleep.

*   *   *   *   *

"Talking never brought the turf home," was one of Kelly the butler's favourite old sayings and so Lucy was determined to formulate a plan of action with Gavin and Ignatius next day. It was so wonderful having Master Ignatius snooze contentedly on her bed.

Of course, Rachel and her friends had seen fit to jeer at him when she had taken him for a stroll through the village down to the strand. "Which of ye's the pig?" Rachel had called out mischievously, "and who's bringing who for a walk?"

She would simply ignore them and they would soon give up, Lucy told herself resolutely. Her plans had to be postponed for a little while early next morning for she was required to play hostess to a middle-aged couple who came to view the house. Her mother had taken herself off to the café a few minutes before. The woman – a solid woman of ample proportions – was dressed in a tweedy jacket and skirt, a brooch with a Celtic motif shining on her lavender blouse. Her husband was small by comparison, his hair visibly thinning on top.

"What a lovely little garden," the woman said. "Of course, our own garden at home is twenty times bigger but we don't need all the room now that Padraig has his job in the Civil Service and Ashling is married to that doctor and Crona is working in Bahrain. What we need now is a small little house, no bigger than a doll's house, and though I'm not very keen on living in a terrace

39

this house seems to be just the right size for myself and Maurice and Fionn. Fionn is our pedigree red setter. And what a lovely little living-room," she continued, as Lucy showed her round with something less than enthusiasm.

"Some of the furniture wouldn't exactly be my taste, oh no, no," the woman went on with more than a hint of snobbery. "But, you know, I think I could do something with this room, I really could." Maurice, who seemed to have taken on the aspect of a pet poodle, followed meekly behind his wife and only spoke when called upon to do so by her.

"Are you sure you wouldn't mind looking straight across the road at the neighbours, or having them look straight across the road into your living-room?" Lucy asked, for she was less than keen on selling the house.

"Yes, that might be a problem, but nothing that couldn't be overcome with better quality net curtains or with a blind," the woman answered pensively. Next came the kitchen and the adjoining utility room. Once again the woman poked her nose into every cupboard and drawer. Once again she found fault with the decor and the woodwork.

"I'm not very keen on laminated surfaces – nothing like the real thing," she sniffed.

When Lucy offered to make a cup of tea for her guests she hoped they would politely decline but they didn't. They said they'd had a long journey and a cup of tea would be very refreshing. They decided to have a stroll round the back garden while the kettle was boiling. Lucy rolled her eyes. She had never met such a pair of pompous twits.

Meanwhile Ignatius had been asked to remain perfectly still under the bed until the prospective buyers had left. However they took a great deal of time over their tea. The lady in the tweed suit gave a lecture on the advantages of herbal tea and lemon tea and so Ignatius, feeling it beneath him to remain so long beneath a bed, duly crept forth from his hiding place and made himself comfortable in the bed. He could hear the woman clucking downstairs – she was like a long-playing record with the needle stuck in the groove but soon Lucy and her guests were climbing the stairs.

"The bathroom is very small but so quaint. Our big bed at home would occupy so much space in the main bedroom and we'd have little or no room for our antique wardrobe and dressing-table – very fine pieces and very valuable, as Maurice will tell you."

Maurice was about to tell her but once again he was cut short in mid-stream. They proceeded to inspect Lucy's brother's room. What a pity Rory was away for when Rory was in residence his bedroom looked for all the world like a pre-war jumble sale. And then came the best moment, her own bedroom. The woman admired the primrose-coloured walls and the matching curtains and quilt. However, she could not help noticing the big bulge under the bedclothes and she became curious about it.

"It's nothing, nothing at all," Lucy assured her with some embarassment but the woman's curiosity was not so readily satisfied.

"There's no need to be embarassed, my dear, I know what it is," the woman insisted as she drew nearer the bed, her husband smiling benignly in the background.

"You know what it is?" Lucy mumbled quizzically.

"Yes, yes, of course, it's a teddy bear, isn't it?" the woman said knowingly. "No need to be embarassed, no need at all. Our Crona had a teddy bear till she was sixteen, as Maurice will tell you." Maurice nodded again. "Now let's see your fine big teddy."

Lucy grimaced. The woman drew back the clothes and gaped in amazement to find a rather smug-looking pig gaping back at her.

"Good morning, dear lady – enchanted to make your acquaintance I'm sure and how may I be of service to you?" the pig asked in his cultured way. The woman seemed lost for words which was an extraordinary occurrence in itself.

"It's a... it's a pig," she stammered, still dumbfounded by the pig's very civil greeting to her. "It's a pig and… and he spoke to me."

"Pray tell, are you feeling quite well, my dear?" Ignatius persisted, revelling in the woman's confusion. "May one recommend a little nap? One has always found a little *siesta* so refreshing when one is upset."

The woman began to sniffle and rummaged in her huge handbag for a handkerchief. Her husband ushered her out of the room as Lucy hurriedly covered Ignatius with the bedclothes once more.

"It's the long journey, I expect. I feel a bit dizzy all of a sudden," the woman explained as she and her husband made their way downstairs. They hastily thanked Lucy for showing them round and told her that they would contact her mother in the very near future to let her know of their decision. When Lucy had said goodbye to her guests, she climbed the stairs once more, a grin of satisfaction on her face. She could guess what their decision would be. "I rather fear I've offended the dear lady. Was it something I said?" said Ignatius and he and Lucy laughed and laughed.

Chapter Four

Only very few people knew that Ignatius could speak. Lucy agreed with him that the fewer people who knew of his secret the better. Later that afternoon, she and Gavin and Ignatius made their way to the fields which had been left to the pig under the terms of MacTaggle's will. Ignatius was worried about his "boater", his elegant straw hat – was it too overstated, he wondered? The will was still the subject of much discussion amongst the villagers. Mr Philbin, the solicitor, was said to be of the opinion that the circumstances surrounding the will were so unusual that it would probably enter the annals of Irish legal history.

"My mum says she doesn't know what all the fuss is about," Gavin said as they ambled along, the sky gloomy and dull overhead.

"While she was waiting at the hairdressers the other day she was reading about this woman in England that left all her jewels to her cat – and a pig is as good as a cat any day."

"One heartily agrees," said Master Ignatius with a swish of his tail. "If a feline can swagger about in diamonds then a pig may lay claim to property." He paused and sucked a mint humbug – nothing like a mint humbug to soothe frayed nerves. "I fear I shall become an addict if this matter is not sorted out very soon," he admitted. "Mint humbugs are all very well after dinner, but one is truly affected when one has to have them so soon after breakfast."

"A few mint humbugs won't do you any harm and you do seem to like them, Ignatius," Lucy told him reassuringly.

"Yes, I like them, but the trouble is I like them too much," Master Ignatius retorted with some anxiety. "One does not take exception to being described as plump but one draws the line at being branded 'chubby' or 'tubby' or something of that nature."

Lucy grinned. Poor Ignatius, he did seem to have some kind of complex about his appearance.

"Have you ever worn jewels, Ignatius?" Gavin intervened,

thinking again of the cat who had been left the jewels by her kind-hearted mistress.

"Oh, yes!" the pig replied with his usual coolness. "Just a little something tasteful and discreet – a little ring to bind my necktie or a gold pocket watch on a chain." He paused and turned to look seriously at Gavin. "Cats, I fear, are something less than discreet in the matter of jewellery. A friend of Hubert's – Miss Wellington – she had a cat, Persephone, such hideously large ear rings, but then she had the ears to hang them."

Lucy grinned again. Ignatius could be so lovably snooty at times.

Lucy and her friends had now decided that they would try and get permission to organise a flag day to raise funds to make improvements in the fields. The most urgent requirement was the building of a shelter. When they arrived at the fields, however, they found a man with a JCB demolishing the timber shack that had served as a temporary shelter for Jasmine. Two signs had been erected. These read "Private Property" and "Trespassers will be Prosecuted". A second man was hard at work setting up posts for the wire and electric fencing he had been ordered to install. Worst of all, the little grey donkey was nowhere to be seen.

Lucy and Gavin and the pig could not believe their eyes and they hurried towards the JCB. "What's going on?" Lucy called out, but the man found it difficult to hear with the noise, and so he switched off the engine for a moment or two.

"Mr MacTaggle's orders," he explained.

"Whose orders?" Lucy wondered in dismay.

"Mr Peregrine MacTaggle's," the driver repeated.

"But this isn't his land!" Lucy insisted.

"I don't know anything about that, girl," the driver replied, clearly anxious to return to his work. "If there's a problem here I suggest you sort it out with the big boss at the Hall."

Lucy glanced quickly about the field, still desperately hoping to catch some glimpse of the lovely little donkey.

"Where's Jasmine? What's happened to her?" she asked with

44

more than a hint of alarm in her tone.

"Jasmine?" the driver repeated quizzically.

"Yes, Jasmine, the grey donkey. She was in this field," Gavin explained.

"Oh, the donkey? Jasmine? Is that her name?" the driver grinned. "Tom Byrne came and took her off. He said she was well enough to go back to work on the strand."

"What?" Lucy cried. "She can't. She'll hurt her leg again."

The driver did not reply. He switched the ignition on again and returned to his work. Master Ignatius felt furious as he and the others made their way out of the field. If they did not take a stand against the grasping Peregrine they would lose the fields forever.

"Abominable behaviour! I will not countenance it!" said Master Ignatius, stomping his right foretrotter indignantly against the ground. "I hope the horrid one chokes on his prunes."

Lucy looked at him quizzically.

"Oh, haven't I told you, my dear? Peregrine is rather partial to prunes." Another pause. "He has the stomach for them, you know."

"Maybe we should tell the guards," Lucy suggested as they hurried along.

"That wouldn't do any good. The guards only get involved when there's a breach of the peace or something," Gavin replied. "The only chance we've got is to go to court and put our case there."

"But we can't afford to go to court, and Peregrine knows that only too well," Lucy sighed. "This is his way of outsmarting us, but what can we do?"

"We can't give up this easily even if we can't go to court," Gavin insisted. They were now walking beside the old perimeter wall of the estate, a wall that had been built a hundred years or more before. "We've got to think of something."

In the meantime, they decided to hurry down to the strand to see if there was anything they could do to help Jasmine. The beach at Ballymactaggle was small but scenic and very sandy. It was a favourite spot for families, for it was generally considered to be one of the safest beaches in Kerry. Marram grass with rush-like leaves grew on the sand-dunes which also provided a home for plants such as the sea holly with its prickly bluish-green leaves. Great fires of fuchsia flamed in the hedgerows of the fields that sloped away from the strand.

There were very few visitors on the beach, the day being dull and cheerless but midway down the beach Rachel was chatting with the boys who looked after the donkeys for her father. As usual she was smoking a cigarette – giving herself airs and graces and putting on funny accents.

"Look! Look! It's Jasmine," Lucy said to Ignatius as they drew near to the little group, the donkeys clustered about them.

"Sorry, luv," Rachel sniggered. "We'd luv to let you take part in our race but no pigs allowed – them's the rules and rules is rules."

"What race?" Lucy demanded angrily.

"Me and Mikey here, we're having a race, luv," Rachel explained in the same sniggering tones. "Mikey on Whiskey Dew and meself on little Miss Jasmine."

The lean and lanky Mikey smirked. Rachel was some menace when it came to putting on an act.

"But you can't race on Jasmine," Lucy said in pleading tones. "The sprain on her leg isn't better and she's still a bit lame."

"Do ya hear that, Mikey luv?" the other girl said with a wink. "'Tis how I'm thinkin' you'll have to be givin' me a headstart." Then she curtsied towards Lucy and Ignatius. "And 'tis hopin' I am ye'er honours will find our little biteen of a race to ye'er likin' for we bein' poor peasants, we don't rightly know how to playse the quality such as ye'erselves." She took another drag of the cigarette and deliberately blew the smoke into Lucy's face. Then turning to the lanky Mikey, she resumed: "Are you right so, Mikey, me darlin', for 'tis time to get the show on the road – for we can't be keepin' the quality from their tay."

Suddenly Lucy grabbed at the reins attached to Jasmine's head, wrenching it free from the grasp of the boy who was holding it.

Next moment she turned and was racing up the strand with Jasmine by her side. Gavin and Ignatius were close behind, Rachel and Mikey and the others in hot pursuit.

Lucy ran like the wind and the gentle Jasmine was only too happy to respond with a surprising fleetness of foot. The light sea breeze swept through Lucy's red hair causing it to float and flame about her shoulders. She just had to get Jasmine away to a place of safety. That was the one overwhelming thought in her mind, the jeers and threats of her pursuers ringing in her ears. Gavin also readily kept up the pace but soon poor Master Ignatius was huffing and puffing. He had never been the most athletic of pigs and his recent addiction to mint humbugs had not helped.

"Grab the pig!" Rachel demanded grimly. The lanky Mikey instantly moved up a gear but though Master Ignatius might never come within an ass's roar of the land speed record, he was by no means a slow coach. Whenever Mikey reached out to grab at him he took evasive action, moving sharply to the right or to the left, causing his pursuer to fall flat on his face more than once. This caused no little merriment amongst his fellows – except Rachel, of course, who become more and more frustrated with each passing second. After some moments she came to the conclusion that if she wanted something done she would have to do it herself. With one ungraceful but determined lunge she caught a firm hold of the pig's head, obliging him to come to a sudden halt.

"Come back with my donkey or the pig gets it!" Rachel called after Lucy and Gavin. Lucy stopped. What should she do? She looked at Gavin but his expression was as blank as her own.

"Bring back my donkey or I'll be posting you a packet of rashers for your supper," Rachel called out again.

Master Ignatius squirmed. A pig of noble breeding that had been reared on white wine and strawberries, might not be such a brave soldier after all if Little Miss Hitler and her cronies set about torturing him. Lucy and Gavin and Jasmine moved slowly back towards Rachel and Mikey and the others. It reminded Ignatius of one of those big scenes in spy movies where one spy was exchanged for another except that in this case it was a donkey being exchanged for a pig.

"No fast moves and no tricks this time," Rachel insisted with the same grimness as before.

Lucy's heart began to pound as she drew nearer and nearer to her enemy. She felt like such a traitor and yet if it were a question of loyalties her first loyalty must be to Master Ignatius, for she was now his legal guardian and he was her ward. She prepared to exchange the reins in her grasp for the lead Rachel had thrown around the pig. However, when Rachel had gained possession of the donkey's reins she flung the lead towards Mikey urging him to go for a ride on the pig's back. Mikey duly obliged and clambered aboard the pig, amidst howls of laughter from his friends.

"Giddy-up," he cried, his long legs dragging along the strand. Mikey was very thin and so it was not a great test of the pig's strength to carry him along but poor Ignatius had never been so humiliated in his entire life. A pig of his breeding and background to be treated like a common swine!

"Such a gross attack on one's dignity!" he told himself resentfully. "Don't they know I've played billiards with dukes and duchesses, yes, and even had the good grace to let some of them win." He shrugged himself determinedly. "So many cucumber and apple salads, so many musical evenings, so many encounters at scrabble and chess, and all come to this!" he told himself again. "To be treated, at last, like a common mule, a laughing-stock for the rabble. I will not stand for it."

"I bet you never had a piggyback on a pig before, Mikey luv," Rachel called out.

The pig's patience grew thinner and thinner. Suddenly out of the blue he dashed towards the incoming waves where he did a quite convincing impression of a bucking bronco and unceremoniously dumped his rider into the water. It was now Lucy and Gavin's turn to laugh as Mikey floundered in the waves and Ignatius came panting back to their side, a smirk of quiet pride in his eyes. Mikey was soaked to the skin. "If you did want to go diving, Mikey luv, you should've brought your diving gear," Rachel teased but Mikey was not amused. Every stitch he had on was sodden and he was in no humour to take part in the planned race.

"Ah, come on, Mikey. Don't be a wet blanket!" Rachel said grumpily. "You can go home and change after we have the race."

Mikey did not feel inclined to yield to these suggestions, however. He wasn't going to catch double pneumonia just to satisfy one of Rachel's whims. Rachel was suitably disgruntled, though she pretended not to be. She was sure she would have won anyway and they could always have their race another day.

"If anything bad happens to Jasmine, Rachel Byrne," Lucy screamed with some determination, "I'm going to telephone the ISPCA in Tralee and before you know it you'll be up before Justice Farrell."

"No, I won't," Rachel retorted with a smirk, "because you'll have no time for making calls. You'll be so busy trying to save that porker from the bacon factory."

Had Rachel made some kind of threat, Lucy wondered anxiously as she and Gavin and Master Ignatius moved away. Gavin was more concerned about what they should do to make a stand against the owner of the Hall.

In about an hour Lucy and Ignatius made their way to the stately home of the MacTaggles for a meeting with Kelly in the old Servants' Hall. Lucy was fascinated by so many things in the room, even the big green timber shutters now drawn back to the sides of the windows.

The room was hopelessly cluttered but it was a very homely clutter. Kelly was delighted to see them and he hoped that Master Ignatius was settling into his new home. It was so strange not having him about the Hall, a hint of regret in the old man's voice, but Master Ignatius' safety was more important than anything else in the whole world. The butler went to the door and peered cautiously up and down the corridor – Peregrine had a nasty habit of appearing when he was least expected and they didn't want the enemy getting wind of their plans. When he was satisfied that the coast was clear, the old man returned to his chair opposite Master Ignatius by the fire.

"What we need is some gimmick to get us a bit of publicity," he told Lucy with great earnestness but though he'd racked his brains all day long he'd been unable to think of anything that might work.

"I think I've got rather an excellent idea!" Master Ignatius announced unexpectedly as he drank heartily from a glass of white wine that the butler had seen fit to take from his new master's cellar.

"Why don't Lucy and Gavin get up a 'Support Your Local Pig' petition? They could go about asking people to sign their names in support of one's claim to those two fields which were willed to one by… " a tremor of sadness, "by my dear friend and master."

"That's a great idea, Ignatius," Lucy enthused. "Don't you think so, Mr Kelly?"

"Not a bad idea at all," Kelly agreed with a smile, "for if you could get enough signatures 'twould show Mr High and Mighty Peregrine that he can't ride roughshod over the pigs of Ballymactaggle."

"And it would be good if we could get some publicity for our petition," Lucy mused in pensive mood, sipping now and then from her glass of orange. "And I think I know just the man who can help us, Jarvis Travers – that's not his real name – his real name's Johnny Teahan. He writes for *The Kerry Sentinel* and he came to school to do a story about our skipathon a few months ago."

"He's rather a fool, I fear," Master Ignatius intervened. "He heard the Hall was haunted one time. Pestered poor Hubert about it incessantly. Oh, Hubert would have filled the fellow full of buckshot if I hadn't intervened." He paused and sipped again. "It was a mercy things didn't develop. The musket, you know rather lacked a sense of direction – it fired backwards instead of forwards."

50

"He might be more trouble than he's worth," Lucy agreed, "but that's a chance we have to take." Next they turned their attention to the drafting of the text which would appear at the top of the petition. After much changing and rearranging of words, they eventually agreed on the following: "We, the undersigned, support Master Ignatius' claim to the two fields bequeathed to him in the will of the late Mr Hubert MacTaggle, and we therefore request Mr Peregrine MacTaggle to acknowledge Master Ignatius as the lawful owner of the fields and to grant him access to his property."

"Brilliant," Lucy enthused with mounting delight. She would ask Julie who worked in the office in Leens' hardware shop to type out the text on a clean sheet of paper and she could also use the photocopier there to make copies. She could count on Gavin to help with the petition and maybe a few more of her friends would help too. They would set about asking for signatures first thing in the morning. Suddenly there was an abrupt and urgent knock on the door and Lucy's heart missed a beat.

"Are you in there, Kelly?"

It was Peregrine's voice. Impulsively Lucy grabbed Ignatius by the foretrotter and dragged him behind the curtains that were frayed with age. The toes of the girl's shoes and the tips of her companion's trotters were barely visible. The butler shuffled in a seemingly unconcerned fashion towards the door and began to sing along the way:

> "Near to Banbridge town in the County Down
> One morning last July,
> Down a boreen green came a sweet coleen
> And she smiled as she passed me by."

"Are you alone? I thought I heard voices?" Peregrine asked suspiciously when he was admitted to the room at last.

" 'Twill be my singing you're after hearing, sir, for Mister Hubert, God rest his soul, used to say I'd a voice like McCormack," the butler told him coyly.

51

"Yes, I can quite see that he might, being tone deaf since the age of three – a fall from his cradle, I believe," Peregrine retorted tartly skimming his eyes across the room. The butler burst into song again in an effort to distract him.

"And what would your own verdict be, sir?" Kelly wondered when he had sung a few more lines.

Peregrine looked at him quizzically. "I mean, your verdict on my singing, sir," the butler elaborated.

"It makes one rather regret they they abolished hanging when they did," Peregrine retorted with the same curtness as before.

"So glad to be appreciated, sir," said Kelly as if he didn't understand, ushering the newcomer towards the door once more.

"Excellent performance!" enthused Master Ignatius when the danger had passed and he resumed his seat by the fire once more. "I trod the boards myself one time, you know."

"You mean you were an actor?" Lucy asked in disbelief.

"Oh, yes, my dear, a diversion for Christmas. Hubert's idea," the pig explained.

"And what did you play?" Lucy persisted.

"A hatstand!" Ignatius retorted with the utmost gravity but Lucy couldn't resist a grin.

"Rather a superior hatstand, of course," the pig assured her before taking another sip of his wine. "One can tell a great deal about an individual's character from his hatstand, you know. Peregrine's is, I fancy, rather lopsided and showy." Lucy grinned again. She was living with the smartest pig in Ireland. Most people read tea leaves but Ignatius read hatstands.

*   *   *   *   *

Lucy's mother was very disappointed when she learned that the possible buyers hadn't seemed very impressed with the house, but it was too soon to give up yet. It was very high-handed of the new man at the hall to put up those private property signs and even though it would have made life a lot easier for all concerned if the pig had decided to hand over the fields and come to a settlement she felt that Master Ignatius was right in not giving in to his enemy's pressure. Nor did she object to the pig petition as long as it did not come to the notice of potential buyers that they were harbouring a pig on the premises. It would hardly be a selling point if it became common knowledge that the house had served as a pigsty. Lucy's father was a little disappointed, too. The work at the Hall would have kept him going for years, unlike his present position, hopping form one little job to the next. But then if a pig has his principles he must stand by them.

Lucy hurried away after supper. She would wash all the dishes another time. She was always saying that, her mother sighed wearily, but now Lucy had to go and find recruits for her pig campaign. Ignatius could stay at home and watch television Indeed Master Ignatius was already seated comfortably in his armchair and was holding the remote control in his right foretrotter. He zapped the control and switched channels for he had seen a paragraph in the paper about a programme on the Russian ballet and he had always been quite keen on the Russian ballet.

"Switch back to the sports quiz," Lucy's father demanded with some impatience for the sight of supple bodies wafting airily about the screen did not appeal to him in the slightest. Master Ignatius, however, did a good imitation of a rock and chose to ignore his companion's trifling contribution. Such grace, such mastery, such technique, he marvelled to himself as the dancers swirled and whirled with such effortless grace. "Such a charming *pas de deux*," he exclaimed at length. "I've rarely witnessed finer."

"Will you cut the foreign lingo, pig? I said I want to see the sports quiz," Lucy's father said with mounting frustration but again his words were charmingly ignored.

"Don't be harassing poor Master Ignatius, Joe" his wife called out from the kitchen. "It won't do you any harm at all to watch a bit of the ballet. It's good to know about these things."

"Woman, give me a break. I've had a long day," Joe answered

53

wearily, "and the least I can expect when I come home in the evening is a half-hour's relaxation in front of the telly."

"I quite like the ballet myself," Lucy's mother announced as she joined the others in the living-room, "and sure Master Ignatius is new in the house, so we'll make him feel at home by letting him decide what we watch on the telly just for tonight. After that you can take turns."

"Most obliged, dear lady, most obliged," the pig replied in his elegant way. "I wouldn't want to miss this for the world for I think we may be watching the new Nijinksky."

"I didn't know they had race horses in the ballet," Lucy's mother replied with some bewilderment and Master Ignatius looked at her in amazement. He was tempted to tell her that Nijinsky had been a ballet star long before he'd been a racehorse but she wouldn't understand. Joe O'Brien said no more. He simply hunched his shoulders in disgust. If this kind of thing got out, he'd never live it down. Playing second fiddle to a pig in his own front room.

Chapter Five

Master Ignatius' lack of fitness on the strand prompted him to rise early next morning, go downstairs and switch on the aerobics programme on television. Soon, on the instructions of the glamourous TV hostess, he was performing the most elaborate and alarming bodily contortions on the living-room floor. The blonde lady in the pink leotard made the exercises seem so easy but they proved more difficult for a largely lazy pig. The bouncy modern music was enough to give any plump porker of distinction a heart problem. However, he simply must continue, he told himself, as he swayed this way and that in his purple satin boxer shorts – a present from MacTaggle the previous summer.

Soon he was perspiring heavily. Polite pigs don't sweat, but there was the consolation that it would be worth all the effort in the end. If he had been a little more nimble on his feet on the beach, Jasmine would probably have made a clean getaway and the fact that she had not, left him feeling just a little guilty. He did not feel in the least bit guilty, however, about the fact that the music from the TV was disturbing the entire household and probably some of the neighbours as well.

"What's that pesky pig up to?" Joe O'Brien wondered with some justification as he glanced at the clock before pulling the bedclothes over his head.

"We'll just have to be patient with him, dear," his wife answered in her motherly way. "After all, he is just a pig and this being his first time away from home, he's probably feeling a bit homesick." She tried hard to remember some of the misery she had experienced on her first few days away from home but that had been a long time ago. The upset of MacTaggle's death had probably unsettled him, too.

"I'll unsettle him for good if he doesn't give over that racket and soon," Joe O'Brien vowed grumpily, but his wife merely smiled, for she knew that in reality he wouldn't hurt a fly. After what seemed like an eternity the racket ceased. The programme came to an end and Ignatius clambered, gasping, upstairs. He would have a hot bath, nothing like a soak in the tub to relieve the tension in the muscles. The trouble came when Ignatius chose to soak himself for so long that no one else could use the bathroom.

"Ignatius," Lucy whispered impatiently. "It isn't nice to hog the bathroom all to yourself and Dad has to go to work soon."

Soon Lucy's mother made her own attempt to woo the pig from the bath. "Ignatius, dear," she said softly with a tentative knocking on the door. "Would you be a dear and try to hurry up?" She listened for a few moments but she could hear nothing, nothing at all. She began to grow alarmed. Surely the poor pig had not... she could scarcely bring herself to translate her thoughts into words... had not drowned in the bath? What would happen if he had? They might have to call in the county coroner to rule out foul play.

She had heard of homicide but never hogicide – except, of course, in a bacon factory. She being one of his next of kin, so to speak, being the mother of his legal guardian ,would have to dress in black for the "obsequies" which was the posh word used for a funeral in papers like *The Irish Times*. She rushed back to the bedroom to tell her husband that she feared Ignatius had "popped his clogs", or in this case, his trotters. During her absence, however, the superior pig clambered nonchalantly from the bath and dried himself with a towel.

"Stand back now, Lily, stand back," Joe O'Brien said to his wife in a tone of some gravity. He would make a run for the door and force it open. He duly rushed headlong at the door which was opened unexpectedly by the pig, with the result that the master of the house did not come to a halt until he toppled onto the toilet seat.

"So sorry to have kept you," said the elegant pig as he sauntered past

Lucy smiled but she had a big day before her. Soon she and Gavin and two other recruits were preparing to set forth to gather support for their pig petition. They had divided the village and the parish into zones so that none of them would duplicate the work of the others.

Before they set forth, however, Lucy, taking on the role of leader, gave her fellow campaigners a final pep talk. If they met with a poor response at the doors they must continue. They must remember that they were fighting for the rights of the average pig in the street. Ignatius did not take too kindly to being described as "an average pig in the street", but he did not intervene. They were fighting to prove that every creature in the country – even a pig – had the right to claim and use any property that was legally his.

When the time came for the members of that stalwart band to move out into the narrow little streets of Ballymactaggle, they felt like the pioneers in the old west breaking new ground in their efforts to ensure that Ignatius might go where no pig had gone before.

Master Ignatius stood by Lucy's side as she knocked on the doors of the houses in the terrace. Such a good-looking, handsome, respectable pig most people said, Yes, of course, they would sign the petition, for it would be a bad thing to go against the last wishes of a fine old gentleman such as the late MacTaggle. One or two of the householders were a little grumpy, however, they had enough problems of their own than to be worrying about the inheritance of a spoiled pig. These people were very much the exception to the rule, however.

The deep blue sky high above was embellished with wisps of candyfloss cloud and Lucy was feeling very encouraged. Master Ignatius could produce such an appealing smile – he was just like a little baby, that almost everyone wanted to cuddle and protect. The barking of tiresome little dogs – such dim-witted creatures – began to worry him, however, as morning edged closer and closer to noon. What did they take him for anyway – a wild boar? Any mutt could see he was the most elegant pig in the parish. Gavin and the others were busy, too, each of them drumming up as much support as they could for their fabulous friend, the pig.

After lunch, Lucy telephoned the news reporter, Jarvis Travers, real name John Teahan, at *The Kerry Sentinel*. A petition in support of the pig? It wasn't exactly earth-shattering stuff but he would come round to do an interview in about half an hour or so.

While they waited in the living-room, Lucy and Gavin flicked through the mass of signatures that they and their friends had collected during the course of the morning. The petition looked very impressive when all the pages were stapled together. If this didn't help Master Ignatius gain possession of his property they didn't know what would.

Ignatius was, however, as he whispered to Lucy, "rather pooped" – trailing about the streets all morning long was not a sophisticated pig's idea of fun. Lucy comforted him by telling him he should try to see their morning's efforts as a battle for the advancement of pigs everywhere. Besides, all that walking would do wonders for his fitness programme. Master Ignatius was not very impressed and now he rested in the armchair and there came upon him a great craving for a glass of white wine.

Travers, who arrived a few moments later, was in his thirties, with neatly groomed mouse-coloured hair, bubbling brown eyes and an infectious smile.

"So, this is the pig of the moment, the trendy pig about town. Pleased to make your acquaintance, kind sir," he said in his friendly way as he swaggered into the living-room, the tail of his light linen coat swirling loosely about him. He removed his coat, tossed it on the sofa, sat beside it and withdrew a notebook from his pocket.

Lucy and Gavin were very excited but they tried not to show it. A good headline made all the difference in stories such as this, Travers assured them as he fumbled in the pocket of his jacket for a pencil.

"Children Rally to Porker's Plight". Yes, that was a good one, or "Pompous Pig in Property Battle".

Travers then proceeded to ask a great many questions about the terms of Hubert MacTaggle's will, about Lucy's role as the pig's legal guardian and about Peregrine's refusal to surrender the fields to the pig.

"We don't want any quarrel with Peregrine," Lucy said. "We just want to make sure that Ignatius is given the land which was willed to him."

"And what does Ignatius intend to do with the property, should he gain possession of it?" the reporter asked, scribbling down notes at a furious pace.

"He wants to set up a shelter for stray and unwanted donkeys," Lucy explained hesitantly for she was reluctant to relate the story of Jasmine's adventures but the reporter pressed the matter further.

"Are there many unwanted donkeys in these parts, then?" he persisted.

"Donkeys are used for rides on the beach and when they get old they will have a home to go to – if the shelter is set up," Gavin intervened.

Lucy smiled. Gavin's answer was a very good one.

"Sometimes there are stories in the newspapers of donkeys being ill-treated or abandoned or simply neglected," Lucy herself continued. "These donkeys too would be welcome at the shelter."

"Will you be able to use the story?" Gavin wondered when all the questions had been asked.

"Oh, sure," the reporter answered, "but, of course, I'll have to visit the Hall to hear the other side of things. There's two sides to every story, as they say."

Lucy frowned. She did not like the sound of that. Who could tell what wholesome gloss Peregrine MacTaggle might put on his refusal to part with the fields to her friend, Ignatius? And despite his air of breezy enthusiasm, the friendly Travers was one who might be easily impressed. Travers would, however, have to take a photograph of the pig before he bade them goodbye. Lucy insisted that they must take the photograph in the back garden – they were trying to sell their house and her mother would kill her if the photograph were taken in the living-room.

"We'll take him down near that ramshackle old stone shed at the bottom of the garden," Travers suggested, as he led the way through the clumps of grass. "It will make him look a bit more destitute – get a bit more sympathy – he'll look the part of a penniless pig, orphaned and abandoned." Master Ignatius looked suitably indignant.

"Ramshackle old shed," Lucy repeated to herself. If only her mother had heard this less than flattering description for she herself had described it as "a multi-purpose outbuilding of great character, suitable for use as a storeroom, workshop or garage".

Ignatius stood before the old stone wall of the outhouse, Travers advising him not to smile but to look "a bit down in the puss" like a pig that had just caught swine fever.

"Oh, very charming. Not only destitute but also diseased," Ignatius mused. What a fall from grace for a pig who had lived in the lap of luxury for so long.

If Lucy and Gavin and the pig had had a busy day, Rachel Byrne had also not been idle. She was always slinking away from the café to play the jukebox in the chip shop or to idle her time with the boys on the strand. This morning, however, she had found time to make a very interesting phone call. She had listened intently as the telephone rang at the other end of the line.

"Good morning, Southern Health Board, can I help you?"

"Martha MacFadden spaykin'," Rachel had begun in a pronounced Kerry accent, "things is come to a terrible state when people are allowed to keep pigs in the parlour again."

The Public Health Officer, a prim, smartly dressed lady in her thirties had said she did not understand.

" 'Tis the O'Briens, I'm spaykin' about, Missus," Rachel had gone on, warming to her subject.

"The O'Briens do live in the terrace beyond – 'tis how they're after takin' a pig into the house to live with them."

"Really!" had been the dismayed response from the other end of the line.

" 'Tis the truth I'm spaykin', Missus," Rachel had insisted. "For 'twould turn wan's stomach to see that dirty ill-gotten pig aytin' his mayles in their kitchen. Oh, indeed, wouldn't it turn the stomach of a donkey to face a pig at breakfast?"

"And are you objecting to the presence of the pig on the premises?" the other voice had enquired politely.

"You may be sure I'm objectin'," Rachel had retorted with the same gusto as before, "for 'tis how I'll be wearin' a clothes peg on my nose if that pig do stay where he is much longer." Then Rachel paused, trying with some difficulty to repress a giggle.

The other voice had then politely thanked her for her telephone call. The woman said she would make no delay in investigating the matter fully and if the situation was as Mrs MacFadden had described, steps would be taken urgently to improve it. "Mrs MacFadden" had then gleefully replaced the receiver, a gloating gleam of triumph in her eyes as she made her way downstairs to the café, anticipating in her mind's eye the nasty shock that lay in store for Lucy O'Brien and that revolting pig.

"You're looking very pleased with yourself this morning," Rachel's father had said when she joined him behind the counter in the café.

"Am I, Dad?" she had replied coyly. "It's just that I've a feeling you won't have to worry about that pig and the plans for a donkey shelter anymore."

"Do you know something I don't know?" her father had asked curiously. He was a portly man with a flabby face that masked that streak of ruthlessness and determination which was very much part of his character. Rachel had not answered but had smiled a knowing smile.

About half past three Ignatius had taken himself upstairs for a late afternoon *siesta*. Hubert had always had a nap about that time – after his walk and before the five o'clock tea and scones. An hour or so later Lucy was reading a book when there came a knock on the door. She opened the door and found the prim, smartly dressed lady from the Health Board who thought it prudent to assume the role of a prospective buyer, having seen the "For Sale" sign in the garden. Lucy was a little embarrassed as her mother hadn't said anything about another caller, but, of course, Ms Finch, for that was the lady's name, could look round the house. Ms Finch, who was dressed in a drab grey outfit with a black bow at the neckline, peered into the living room.

"Do you keep any pets?" she wondered casually as she cast a glance of seeming disapproval at the rather brash ornaments on the mantelpiece.

"Oh, n..no," Lucy stammered as convincingly as she could. "We did have a cat one time, but that was long ago."

They moved into the kitchen. Meanwhile upstairs the pig yawned and stretched himself. There was nothing like forty winks to refresh the mind and the body. Then he had a great idea. He would explore Lucy's brother's room and tripped lightly across the corridor and entered Rory's bedroom.

Here were posters of soccer stars – Keane and Quinn and Townsend – and pop stars and streamlined motorbikes. Here, too, was a guitar on top of the wardrobe. Having clambered onto some boxes which he had stacked on a chair, the pig struggled to grab hold of the guitar but just as the guitar seemed to be within his grasp the boxes swayed beneath him and he tumbled to the floor. Luckily neither the noble pig nor the guitar suffered any serious injury, but there had been a terrible crash. The contents of the boxes, marbles and comics and magazines and bits of lego, board-games and trains and space invaders and ghoulish mutants, spewing forth all over the floor.

Ms Finch pricked her ears in the manner of an alert dalmatian, but with a shrug of her shoulders Lucy tried to pass the clatter off as a matter of little importance. She couldn't prevent Ms Finch from charging straight upstairs, however. She would murder Ignatius if he got her into more trouble she told herself with mounting alarm. She tried to divert Ms Finch into her own bedroom but Ms Finch was not so easily diverted and so with a kind of grim determination she directed her steps towards the door of Rory's bedroom. When she opened the door, however, she found the curtains closed and the room in darkness. A darkened form, wearing a dark woolly cap and draped in a rug sat in an armchair that faced towards the window.

Ms Finch moved to examine the figure in the chair more closely but Lucy held her back.

"It's my brother," she whispered in hushed tones. "He's got chickenpox, covered in a rash and a bit feverish at times. Sometimes he thinks he's a... " A pause, the tone becoming more secretive still. "He thinks he's a pig!"

"Good heavens!" replied Ms Finch compassionately. "The poor child. Has he had professional help? It isn't right to have him locked up in a darkened room like this."

"But he likes it like that because other times he thinks he's a mushroom," Lucy lied, her heart drumming with incredible intensity as she thought of just how absurd her story was... a pig with chickenpox!

Ignatius thought it wise to produce a theatrical grunt or two, even though he regarded grunting as a quite degrading practice entirely. Grunting and belching were such vulgar pastimes but now a little pleasant grunting would add weight to Lucy's story about her sadly demented bother – who was in reality at that very moment making faces behind the teacher's back at the Irish College in the Gaeltacht.

"A sad case," Ms Finch mused with the same compassion as before, "but I still say it isn't right making the child spend his time in a darkened room. I'll open the curtains and the sunlight will cheer him up."

Ms Finch moved forward a step or two but Lucy clung to her forearm with the grasp of a drowning swimmer.

"No, you musn't," the girl pleaded, "he's got sore eyes, too. The soreness won't last long, the doctor says, but in the meantime the curtains must stay closed."

There seemed to be something fishy – or was it something piggy – about Lucy's story, the woman thought but what if it were true? Chickenpox was a fairly contagious disease and it would be foolish to take unnecessary risks. It was just possible that Mrs MacFadden, who had sounded like an elderly lady, had heard of the poor boy's delusions about being a pig and had got the wrong end of the stick, or in this case, the trotter.

"Poor, poor boy," Ms Finch sympathised as she took one last lingering look at the figure in the chair and turned to leave the room.

"You must tell your mother, Lucy, if there's anything I can do to help, she musn't hesitate to contact me."

"You won't tell anyone about my brother's condition, will you?" Lucy pleaded. "My mum wouldn't like it and the doctor says it's just a phase he's going through... "

"Of course, I quite understand, dear," the woman assured her when they reached the bottom of the stairs. "You can count on me to be very discreet."

Then she bade her hostess goodbye and as she walked down the garden path she cast a furtive glance at the rose-bushes that were heavily laden with the loveliest blooms. Dear old Mrs MacFadden was surely a bit crazy in her old age.

Lucy placed her back against the door and heaved a sigh of relief. She could just imagine what Rory would say if he heard that she had portrayed him as a fellow who thought he was a pig. But as Kelly, the butler, sometimes said "Any port (or porker) in a storm."

Chapter Six

Lucy and Ignatius took their pig petition to the Hall next day and although Peregrine accepted it from them he promptly slammed the door in their faces.

" 'Tis how he's ragin' with ye for ringin' up that fella Travers," Kelly the butler explained when they made their way round to the old Servants' Hall. "Of course, he plied Travers with drink and 'tis likely he spun some yarn for him for he kept him an age inside in the drawing-room."

All they could do was wait and see what appeared in the paper and hope for the best, the old man added. Then he asked Lucy to play a jig on the accordion. When she obliged he was pleased to see that Master Ignatius began to look a little more spirited and lively.

"One is grieved that one is no longer allowed access to the drawing-room," Ignatius mused. "For there is something rather homely and reassuring about a little tinkle on the piano now and then."

This was news to Lucy who had not known that her favourite pig had felt the loss of the piano so keenly. He could surely afford to buy one from his monthly allowance but the trouble was they had so little room at home. This was the first time in her life she had ever wished they had more space at home – and the pig was not impresssed when it came to keyboards – "electronic gimmicks" was his verdict on them.

"A piano for the pig? 'Tis how you must be jokin' me!" Lucy's mother exclaimed when she broached the subject with her as they prepared some rhubarb for a tart.

"But Ignatius can play really well, can't you, Ignatius?" Lucy said, glancing at the pig who was just at that moment looking through the financial columns of the paper. This was another of Hubert's old customs he found hard to relinquish.

"One has never been a boastful pig," he replied with his usual grace, "but one can play Chopin and Mozart tolerably well."

"Your father wouldn't hear of it, Lucy, and besides, where would we put it? We wouldn't be able to draw one leg after the other if we put it in the living-room," her mother reminded her.

The notion of a piano in the house did secretly appeal to her, however, for she had always believed that a piano lifted the tone of a house – like a nice gnome in the front garden. God only knew that the tone of their house could do with some lifting now that they had a pig in the family. Lucy seemed to have the perfect solution. They could transform "the multi-purpose outbuilding" at the bottom of the garden into a music room for Ignatius and they could have the piano easily delivered through the back garden gate.

Lucy's mother paused and reflected on this suggestion before returning to her task of chopping the stalks of rhubarb into tiny pieces. She glanced long and hard at the old shed. A music room. It had a nice ring to it and it would so impress everyone at the café if she just happened to mention from time to time that she had left her daughter and her friend practising the piano in the music room. Of course, she would have to be especially careful not to spoil the effect by mentioning that her daughter's friend was a pig.

If she set up a few pot plants here and there she could go one better and call it "the conservatory". A spoon fell into the sink and the harsh jangle brought her back to reality. The house was still on the market and her mother needed someone to help her with the household chores. Besides, how on earth could they afford the luxury of a piano when they found it hard enough to pay the light bill?

"But I've spoken to Mr Philbin, the solicitor, on the phone," Lucy persisted. "He says that Ignatius would have no trouble paying for a piano."

"All right, I'll mention it to your father and we'll see what he thinks," her mother replied as she prepared to roll out the dough for the tart and Lucy grinned a radiant grin.

When Lucy and Ignatius went for a stroll – a promenade,

Ignatius called it – they met Gavin walking along the street and he had some interesting news.

"Tom Byrne's bought a new donkey. I think she's called Fuchsia," he told his friends.

"That doesn't sound good for Jasmine," Lucy retorted with some apprehension. Ignatius listened intently but as always maintained a dignified silence in this very public place.

"I heard him giving out about Fuchsia in the cafe. He was like a bull. 'Won't do a thing she's told,' he said, but he'll show her who's boss."

Now Lucy looked even more worried than ever.

"Let's go down to the beach and have a look at her," she suggested at once.

"I've already been there. She isn't there – Mikey jeered at me as always," Gavin replied.

"Well, she must be in Byrne's field then," Lucy suggested. "I'm dying to see what she looks like."

"Poor dear," Master Ignatius observed at length as they drew near the field. "One fears that having Tom Byrne for a master is rather like having a scorpion as one's bosom friend."

Lucy could scarcely resist a grin.

"I've always had a thing about spiders, you know, ever since I was a piglet in the cradle," the pig elaborated. Lucy tried hard to remain serious as she pictured Ignatius in his little baby cap and gown. How his mother must have doted on him – he might even have had a nanny, though whether she had acted the goat or not was open to question.

"And yet it seems frogs regard spiders as something of a delicacy – sometimes one wonders about the sanity of frogs."

"Oh, frogs aren't so bad. In fact I think I like them," Lucy told him seriously.

Ignatius paused and looked at her with some bewilderment. "Just think, my dear – all that hopping about on water lilies – one has to have one's doubts about their state of mind."

Soon they heard the sound of a harsh disgruntled voice coming towards them from the field. It was Rachel's voice and when they came to the rusted gate at last they saw her make valiant attempts to remain aboard the indignant Fuchsia. Rachel scarcely noticed them for a few moments but then she glared at them angrily. She had been certain that after her telephone call to the Southern Health Board that impostor of a pig would be well on his way to the bacon factory by now. And Lucy O'Brien making herself out to be a real goody-goody – getting everyone to sign a petition. It was enough to make a body throw up.

"Clear off, ye pig luvvers!" Rachel screamed at them, her mount doing all in her power to grant her the pleasure of aerial flight.

"Such a delightful person! Such charming manners!" Master Ignatius muttered under his breath and Gavin giggled. Still the spirited little brown donkey kicked and bucked, raising her hind legs high now and then in an effort to dislodge her rider. Rachel clung to the reins in desperation but soon she was flung helplessly to the ground.

"Ooh, I'll get you," she insisted with gritted teeth and remounted once more.

"The trouble with some people is they can never take no for an answer," Ignatius whispered again.

Still Fuchsia stiffened her legs and arched her back, jumping up and down resentfully with more than a little style.

"Giddy up! Giddy up! Do you hear me?" Rachel screamed vindictively now and then but it wasn't too long before she was floored once more.

"It's becoming a bit of a habit," Gavin called out from the gateway.

"You can jeer!" Rachel snapped resentfully, "but you'll be pleased to hear that Dad says as soon as this one's in shape, Jasmine gets the bullet." Then she smirked haughtily and glared at Fuchsia once more. "I wonder how Jasmine will taste as cat food. That's what they do with dead donkeys, you know."

"You're so mean, Rachel Byrne," Lucy retorted. "It's you that should be made into cat food, only no one would bother. You'd turn the stomach of every cat in Kerry."

"I'm sure my cat will fancy a bit of Jasmine," Rachel persisted, delighted with the way in which her vision of the future had annoyed the others. "She isn't too particular in that line, you know. And you can tell your smelly pig if he behaves I might even offer him a tin or two – as a gesture of friendship, like."

"Smelly pig!" Ignatius told himself with mounting anger, "when one has never set foot beyond one's house without bathing one's person in oil of rosemary or sandalwood. In fact, one smells so sweetly one might pass for a rosebush amongst the near-sighted and the bewildered."

Soon Rachel mounted once more only to be ditched yet again. Still she persisted time after time. The watchers at the gate were scarcely aware of it when suddenly Rachel's father came upon them, jostling them aside and striding towards Fuchsia and her crestfallen rider. In a moment he was grabbing the reins and was preparing to bring the whip he held in his hand down on the animal's back. Lucy and Gavin and Ignatius gaped in horror.

"I'll put you in your place, madam, if it's the last thing I do," said the man with the flabby face with a sternness that sent shivers racing down Lucy's spine.

Next moment the terrified Fuchsia felt a searing lash of the whip against her back and she shivered with pain, braying pitifully and struggling to break free.

On impulse Gavin went racing towards Tom Byrne.

"Stop! Stop! Don't hurt her!" he screamed and the passion in his tone was clearly audible but Byrne paid no need to him and brought down a second lash against the donkey's back.

"Stop it! Stop it! You'll kill her! You'll kill her!" Gavin screamed more angrily still and in a moment he was grappling with the man, struggling to wrest the whip from his hand. Rachel observed the struggle with more than a little smugness.

"Mind your own bloody business, boy. It's plagued I am with do-gooders like you," the man roared at him, the light of rage blazing in his eyes. "It's getting to the stage where a man can't do a hand's turn without having some crank knocking on his door."

He shoved the boy from him with a powerful thrust of his hand and Gavin fell backwards onto the grass but though Gavin was down he was by no means out. A moment later he was grappling again with Tom with a fierce strength that belied his seemingly weak appearance. Lucy grimaced and clenched her fingers unconsciously. Gavin's heart pounded with a fury he had never known before. It was as if his entire being had become one overwhelming surge of passion and power.

"You've more fight in you than I gave you credit for," Tom scowled again, "but you'll be sorry you crossed me, boy!"

Still they wrestled with one another like David and Goliath, gasping and panting all the while. Suddenly Gavin snatched the whip from the other's grasp, snapping the rod in two and tearing the lash from it with unbelievable passion. Then he fled from the field, his heart still pounding furiously and though Byrne was tempted to follow him a little distance he gave up after only a few strides, huffing and puffing like a steam train.

"Go after him, Dad! Go after him! Wring his rotten little neck!" Rachel urged, her mouth pouting.

"Never fear, girl, I'm make him sorry yet," her father vowed and she could hear the grimness in his tone.

Now Gavin and his companions were plunging headlong down the road, the pig struggling to keep pace with the boy and the girl and again regretting his recent addiction to mint humbugs. He really must have his exercise bike changed one day soon. It was having no impact on his fitness at all and his aerobics programme was proving equally useless.

"Now I've really gone and done it!" Gavin gasped at last when they came to a halt behind a shed in the laneway.

"I thought you were brilliant. Didn't you, Ignatius?" Lucy retorted with genuine enthusiasm.

"Absolutely splendid! The stuff of heroes and all that!" Ignatius agreed. "If one had it in one's gift to make you a Sergeant Major or some such, one should be only too pleased to do so."

"But don't you see. Now Byrne will hate Jasmine and Fuchsia more than ever," Gavin replied in ominous tones. "He'll take his revenge out on them sooner or later and there isn't a thing we can do about it."

"Don't worry, we'll think of something," Lucy encouraged, scarcely convinced herself.

Later than evening at supper, Lucy's mother mentioned the pig's craving to have a piano of his own. A piano for a pig! Lucy's father had heard it all and he almost choked on his spaghetti.

"Oh, but Ignatius is very musical," Lucy's mother assured him. "He dances when Lucy plays the accordion and he loves all those fancy culture programmes on television – you know the ones where they all sound as if they're talking with marbles in their mouths."

Lucy's father sighed and put his hand to his forehead.

"Next you'll be telling me he wants to compose his own opera," he said with a good-humoured smile. "He could call it 'The Prize Porker of Ballymactaggle' by Ignatius O'Pig. "

Mrs O'Brien paused a moment and took a potato from the dish which had been passed ever so politely to her by the pig.

"Now, there's a good idea," she resumed with enthusiasm. "Have you ever thought of writing an opera or a ballet of your own Ignatius? A pig of your talents would have no problem with such a thing, I'm sure."

"I must admit the notion has crossed my mind from time to time, dear lady, but one has had so many other preoccupations of late," the pig replied quickly, as he delicately manipulated his knife and fork. "I had rather thought of something along the lines of a superior musical – something to appeal to all. "

Suddenly Lucy's father began to burst out laughing and the laughter was uncontrollable for a few moments. Lucy grinned too.

"Oh, you fancy I couldn't do it, do you?" Ignatius asked with sudden indignation when Lucy's father had regained his composure.

"Oh, I'm sure you could," Joe O'Brien said mischievously. "And you could write such classics as 'I Left my Pig in San Francisco', or

'The Hog I Loved So Well', or 'I'm Just a Pig in a Poke'."

"You may titter, sir," Ignatius said gravely, "but I see no reason why a musical about pigs should not be a resounding success. Pigs are as fascinating as felines any day of the week."

"Ah, Dad, stop teasing Ignatius," Lucy intervened. "What does it matter whether he can write a musical or not? He loves the piano and we should get him one."

It took some time to persuade Lucy's father that a piano would be good for Ignatius. He was told that the pig could afford to pay for it himself and that there would be more than enough room for it in "the multi-purpose outbuilding of some character" – the shed at the bottom of the garden. However, Joe O'Brien was finally persuaded. Lucy jumped for joy but the pig's response was more reserved. Now he had something to prove and he would prove it.

* * * * *

Gavin was in a thoughtful mood as he sat in the living-room of the modest bungalow where he lived with his mother and brother. His brother Nick was much older than he – eighteen to be exact.

Leather and denim were his trademarks and he was into everything from heavy metal to soccer. His passion, however, was motorbikes and, working in the local garage, he had come across an old crock which he had transformed into the most fabulous machine on earth.

There were times when Gavin envied him his freedom. Their mother always treated Nick like an adult and she didn't nag him half as much about wearing this or that jumper or jacket. His own relationship with Nick had always been "delicate" – that seemed to be the way of the world when it came to brothers. But to make matters worse he had been playing about with Nick's motorbike a few days before and had managed to knock it sideways, denting it noticeably in the process. In reality it had only been a small dent but even a small dent was a major disaster as far as Nick was concerned. Now, however, the germ of an idea was forming in

Gavin's mind and when his brother came in from the yard he broached it with him at last.

"I want to rescue Fuchsia and Jasmine and take them away from Tom Byrne," he announced abruptly, fidgeting with the animal book he held in his hand. He was always reading about animals, his mother said.

The dark-haired, dark-eyed Nick looked at him in blank amazement.

"Are you cracked? Are you after getting a bang on the head or what?" his brother retorted with deadly earnestness.

"Please, Nick, please. You've got to help me," Gavin pleaded. "He's only letting Jasmine live as long as Fuchsia plays up and when Fuchsia comes into line he'll shoot poor Jasmine."

"Look, Gav, old boy, Tom Byrne is a pain as far as I'm concerned," his brother assured him, "he likes to throw his weight around when it comes to animals and people alike. He wears his arrogance like an old suit of clothes but it's more than my job's worth to get involved."

"But how would he know who was involved if we made off with the donkeys in the middle of the night?" Gavin persisted. He was like that when he got something into his head. "We could bring them to grand uncle Matty's place up in the mountains. That's out of the way entirely and no one would be any the wiser."

"Don't you listen to anything I say?" his brother protested. "If Tom ever found out who took his donkeys it wouldn't be just Jasmine getting the bullet, it would be me getting the bullet from my job – and me and you up before Justice Farrell in the morning. And what would that do to Mum? Think about that, sunshine!"

"But you didn't see the way he was whipping Fuchsia," Gavin insisted. "It was the cruellest thing you ever saw. I've got to get them away from him, I've got to and I can't do it on my own."

"No, Gav, I said no. Count me out of this one and take a word of warning. Tread warily, sunshine, tread warily," his brother insisted flatly and Gavin returned to his book in despair.

Chapter Seven

Master Ignatius' legal guardian telephoned Mr Philbin, the solicitor, next day asking him if he would kindly purchase a piano for her ward. Furthermore, it was to be delivered to the terraced house, or more precisely to the garden shed as a matter of urgency. Mr Philbin was only too happy to oblige for, as he said quite openly, he had always found Master Ignatius a most sociable and charming pig.

Later that night, Lucy and Gavin, Gavin's brother Nick and Master Ignatius were creeping silently through the darkened streets of Ballymactaggle. The tension was almost palpable now and when the old church clock began to clang in its ancient tower, beating out the chimes, one, two, three, Lucy's heart missed a beat.

Gavin had, at length, through a mixture of flattery, pleading and begging, enlisted the support of his brother in his bid to rescue the donkeys and now they were hurrying towards the garage where Nick had left a van and a trailer in readiness.

"There are times when one can quite see that being a cat has its advantages after all," said Master Ignatius ruefully. He had just had the misfortune to make close and unwelcome contact with yet another flowerpot for what seemed like the zillionth time. "Night vision, you know, my dear, but when one is a pig I fear one takes as much pleasure from a night-time jaunt such as this as a frog exploring a minefield.

"Ssh, ssh, Ignatius," Lucy urged in whispering tones, helping him to his feet. Even her own whispers added to her unease.

"On the other hand," the pig retorted blithely, "cats have such strange obsessions. One cannot quite see the merit of making a career of the destruction of mice when mousetraps come so cheap."

"Will someone tell the pig to put a sock in it?" Nick demanded impatiently and Ignatius, looking suitably offended, was silent again. They came to the van at last and scrambled on board, Lucy's heart beating with the same disquiet as before, the dread in

74

Gavin's eyes a reflection of her own. It would be bad enough getting themselves into trouble but they'd never forgive themselves if Nick lost his job. The stillness was cloying now. It felt almost tangible as if it might be grabbed and tightened and squeezed in the hand.

"This rather reminds one of an old Humphrey Bogart movie," Ignatius observed with unexpected relish. "Heroes to the rescue and all that sort of thing."

Nick rolled his eyes in despair. Why, oh why, had he allowed the pesky pig to tag along?

"One was always a fan of Bogart and Garbo, you know. Garbo had such heavenly eyes. One could almost have swooned at their Swedish appeal."

"I didn't think you went in for that sort of thing," Lucy replied, forgetting herself for a moment.

"Oh, I quite see what you mean, my dear," Ignatius replied in his superior way, "but one must admit one did have visions of oneself fleeing with Garbo on some rickety train into the snowy landscape of tomorrow." He paused and stifled a sigh of regret. "And when she fell – fur coat and all – into the hero's arms, the hero would be me."

Lucy grinned. Poor Ignatius. He did allow his imagination to run wild at times.

They came, at last, to the field which was visible from the first floor bedroom above the café, the windows of which were now cloaked in darkness. Lucy's heart pounded as it had never pounded before.

"The pig stays put in the van," Nick insisted and Ignatius looking mortally wounded merely shrugged his shoulders. In a moment the others were opening the rusted gate as noiselessly as they could, but it cranked loudly on its hinges. There were six or seven donkeys in the field but they couldn't rescue them all. Besides apart from the frisky Fuchsia and the ageing Jasmine, Tom Byrne was having no major difficulties with the others, at least not for the time being.

"Kidnapping donkeys!" Nick sighed as if he could scarcely believe that he had been persuaded to lend his support to this reckless scheme. As they moved through the field, the donkeys began to trot about restlessly, eyeing them suspiciously.

"Here, Fuchsia! Here, Jasmine!" Gavin urged in reassuring tones, holding out little lumps of sugar. Jasmine hesitated only a moment or two, then came towards him with familiar confidence as if she recognised his voice as that of a friend. She chewed the sugar from the palm of his hand and he led her quietly towards the trailer. Fuchsia's experience of people, especially in the person of Byrne, had made her more wary than ever and no amount of whispered reassurance on Gavin and Lucy's part could entice her to accept the sugar.

"We'll have to leave her! We can't hang around here all night!" Nick suggested impatiently, glancing towards the darkened café in the distance every now and then.

"No, no, we just can't leave her," Gavin insisted. Ignatius observed the proceedings with some amusement and more than a little disdain.

"We only want to help you, Jasmine," Lucy pleaded in soothing tones, her nerves racing.

"Come, girl, come," Gavin urged again and again, all to no avail.

"Might one be allowed to offer one's services?" asked Ignatius with a coolness that made Lucy's heart miss a beat. Nick wiped the perspiration from his forehead, for the pig becoming impatient at last had left his place in the van.

"I thought I told you to… " Nick began, but his offering was cut short when the pig began to speak with his usual charm to the little brown Fuschia.

"Now, come along, my dear, we are your friends, we have come to take you to a safe place," he began with unexpected mellowness. "You will come to no harm. I give you my word on that and a pig's word is his bond."

Now for the first time Fuchsia stood still and had all the

appearance of listening intently to everything that was said.

"We four-legged ones, we must stand shoulder to shoulder, you know, and keep our colours flying high."

Lucy and her companions gaped in amazement. Again Lucy had visions of Ignatius leading his troops to victory. The strangest thing of all was the fact that Fuchsia did not seem in the least put out by the spectacle of a talking pig even if she didn't understand the sense of his words, she seemed reassured at last.

Nick scratched his head in disbelief as Ignatius led Fuchsia to the trailer and Lucy sighed with relief when they were driving away from the scene of the drama.

"One has always been of the opinion that donkeys are most intelligent creatures," Ignatius observed with quiet pride, "especially when one makes use of a little psychology."

Nick sighed again. One moment the pig was General Franco, now he was Sigmund Freud.

On and on they drove through the lonely country roads, the landscape all about them silent and still. The narrow ribbon roads wound this way and that, up hills and down hills. The majestic mountains, strewn with rocks and hollies became larger and larger all the while, white threaded streams tumbling here and there. The farmhouses and cottages grew more and more scattered until at last there were scarcely any visible at all.

Suddenly the moon emerged triumphantly from the clouds, like a lantern lifted from its place of hiding behind a curtain. Ignatius gasped in amazement at the massive rocks that littered the mountain slopes and then at last, at the end of a long wooded hillside, a farmhouse came into view. Soon Jasmine and Fuchsia were being herded into a field of coarse but sweet grasses and they began to graze with relish for the scraggy pastures in Byrne's field had been cropped almost to the roots.

"Safe at last!" Lucy sighed with satisfaction, for she knew, or at least hoped, that Tom Byrne would never find them here. Nevertheless, she shuddered to think what his reaction would be when he discovered the donkeys were gone.

"Good grief! Do my eyes deceive me?" exclaimed Ignatius with such disgust that Lucy's heart began to drum again, for she thought they had been followed. What had attracted Ignatius' attention, however, was not an angry pursuer but five or six pigs staggering about the roadway.

"Are those pigs intoxicated?"

Nick and Gavin began to titter. Good old grand uncle Matty had been brewing the poteen again and somehow the pigs had managed to help themselves. The drunken ones lurched closer still.

"Drunken swine!" persisted Ignatius with the same indignation as before. "Such clumsy waddling, such unseemly grunting! Have they no pride at all?"

"You're right, Ignatius," Nick laughed. "They've hit the bottle in a big way."

"Hit the bottle?" repeated the pig in disdain. "Hit the barrel would be more like it! One's feelings have never been so offended in one's life."

"Have you never been drunk, Ignatius?" Lucy asked as they returned to the van.

"Certainly not, my dear," retorted Ignatius as if the question was absurd. "One has been tipsy, merry and so forth, but one has never been intoxicated to the point of being legless."

Nick laughed again and Gavin grinned as they gave one last look at the pigs swaying about the roadway.

Next day Tom Byrne laboured under the illusion that his donkeys had merely strayed and would soon be found. Lucy spent much of the day making space in the multi-purpose outbuilding for the much desired piano. Gavin helped her. He was intrigued by the decision of the O'Briens to buy a piano and as he suspected he soon discovered that it was intended for the benefit and pleasure of their cultured guest, Master Ignatius. Lucy's mother had had a letter from her own mother that morning – just before she had gone off to the café and though she wouldn't tell Lucy what was in the letter she seemed a bit upset by it.

"I thought the reason you were selling your house was that you could all go and live with your Gran," Gavin said in wondering tones as he struggled to flatten and stuff yet more and more cardboard boxes into a plastic fertiliser bag, which would then be carried to the dump two miles or so from the village.

"Mum got this notion that her mother needed looking after when Granny slipped and sprained her wrist," Lucy explained. "But, as my dad says, 'Granny's fierce independent and she's not likely to die of a sprained wrist.' "

"And what about your Gran? Does she want you to move in with her?"

"No way. She likes being on her own because she has plenty of friends and plenty of company all around her." Lucy said. "And my dad sometimes jokes that the only reason Mum wants to go and live with Gran is to make sure she's home by ten every night."

Lucy and Gavin worked long and hard disposing of unwanted rubbish, arranging and rearranging old discarded presses and cupboards, cramming them to the brim with tools, paint tins and brushes, old pots and pans and kettles and as Kelly the butler might say, "whirlygigs of wan sort or another".

It was just as well that they had worked so hard, cleaning and sweeping and tidying for just before supper, the very same evening, the piano arrived.

Ignatius was very excited but some of the neighbours were more than a little bewildered as they peered discreetly through their respectable net curtains at the huge delivery van that had just come to a halt in the narrow street. What on earth had Lily O'Brien bought, they wondered with mounting curiosity and they couldn't believe their eyes when the delivery men proceeded to remove a huge piano, the men struggling to carry it up the nearby laneway and into the O'Brien's back garden.

"Well, that Lily O'Brien always had to go one step better than her neighbours," a plump woman at the window across the way mused resentfully. "It wouldn't do her at all to get a nice daycent tin whistle for her daughter. No, no, that would be much too common. She had to go the whole hog, she had to get a piano, if you playse," And the ears would be drummed off them for it would be nothing but the piano this and the piano that for days and days and days.

Ignatius could not conceal his joy and the delivery men had scarcely taken their leave of the newly-styled music room when he sat at the piano and began to play a little something for the entertainment of his new family. Indeed he was already feeling so much at home in the O'Brien household that he had come to regard himself as one of the family.

Lucy's mother looked and listened in blank amazement as the little elegant toes on the pigs foretrotters seemed to skim over the keys, producing the most musical tones she had heard in years.

"Oh, the memories this brings back," the pig enthused when he had finished this first performance. "Oh, the treasured memories of those happy times with Hubert in the drawing-room, especially the snowy Christmases when the flames danced in the hearth. I played the piano and Hubert smoked his cigars and drank his brandy and his maiden sister Kitty – large, chubby and dressed in black as if she were always hoping for the pleasure of a funeral – lolled on the sofa and snored her head off."

"Oh, you make it all sound so nice, so very nice," Lucy's mother enthused in her best telephone accent, "and it will be so nice for Lucy to have a pig of your distinction to teach her her music."

"Too kind, dear lady, too kind," said Ignatius graciously.

"And Lucy, if she likes, can call her tutor a swine without telling a word of a lie," her father grinned, but the pig was so taken with his new piano that he wasn't in the least offended by these good-humoured remarks. He would be happy to give Lucy a lesson from time to time, but now he must set to work in earnest on his pig musical which would also be his big musical. And then the pig played another piece, something bright and breezy and cheerful to celebrate the coming of the piano. It really was a beautiful piano, golden-coloured wood polished and gleaming and reflecting his image.

"One does not wish to sound ungrateful but one shall need a more elegant piano stool if one is to proceed with one's musical," the pig said, looking with something approaching distress at the upturned orange crate beneath him.

After a little while Lucy and her parents took their leave of the pig in the music room and returned to the kitchen for their supper. The newest member of the family was much too excited to think of anything so boring as food at that particular time. While they were having supper Lucy's mother mentioned the letter she had received from her own mother.

"You won't believe what she's gone and done," she went on as if horrified by some of the contents in the letter. "I think she must've had a blow to her head that time she fell and hurt her wrist."

"Are you going to tell us what she said in the letter or aren't you? Or are you going to make a ten-part serial out of it, as usual?" her husband asked with a grin.

"I wouldn't mind, but to think that I went to the trouble of putting the house on the market out of the goodness of my heart, so that we could go and live with her and be there when she needed us."

"Are you sure you hadn't a few reasons of you own for wanting to move in with her?" Lucy's father asked. "You said you were sick of Tom Byrne and his café, sick of this pokey little house, sick of the gossip you were hearing down the village – and you still haven't told us the terrible thing your mother's done."

"She's gone and taken in a lodger – a *male* lodger if you please," Lily O'Brien retorted indignantly. "A nice respectable retired gentleman – English he is and a perfect stranger and he has lovely manners but for all she knows he could be the biggest swindler this side of Cork."

"And for all you know he could be the nice polite gentleman your mother says he is. After all your mother isn't some silly sixteen-year-old with a crush on some pimple-sprinkled schoolboy."

Lucy said nothing. She had learned from past experience

81

that it was wiser not to get involved in discussions about her grandmother.

"I've a good mind to drive down there and tell her how ridiculous she is," Lucy's mother insisted peevishly.

"It seems to me you're upset just because your mother isn't in a mood to be pampered," her husband went on with the same frankness. "And while you're down there telling her how ridiculous she is, why don't you tell her how we've lately adopted a talking pig who spends his evenings playing the piano in the shed."

"You're not being serious, Joe," the woman of the house replied indignantly. "You haven't heard the rest of the story. Her lodger is teaching her to drive. Driving at her age!"

"What's so awful about that, Lily?" her husband asked in a more serious mood. "You know as well as I do she's been going on and on for years about how sorry she was she never learned to drive – and if this lodger is the villain you suspect you can be sure your mother, being the shrewd woman she is, will soon see through him."

"I suppose there's no good reason for us to move in with her now," Lucy's mother concluded as she rose from the table. "No good reason to leave this house, so I'd better telephone the estate agent and tell him we've changed our minds."

Lucy was delighted with this development but she was sad for her mother's sake too, because her mother was clearly disappointed at how things had turned out.

"Cheer up, Lily," her husband urged. "Ballytaggle isn't such a bad place and how many families can boast of having a musical pig under their roof?"

Lucy grinned and her mother smiled. At least she would have the consolation of doing up the conservatory and of putting one or two people firmly in their place when she told them about the new piano. It was a good job they hadn't cast aside those wooden framed windows when they put in the new ones a few years before. A good job they had fitted two of them into the shed for now she would have the pleasure of making up curtains for them so that Master Ignatius would be able to compose and play in complete privacy. To tell the truth she was really quite attached to Master Ignatius. She had the most stimulating conversations with him – about art and music and hybrid roses and unlike Hubert and, unlike another person in the room who would be nameless, he didn't snore in this sleep. Joe O'Brien rose and gave his wife a hug.

"I don't snore, do I, Lily?" he asked mischievously.

"Don't snore! You must be joking!" his wife retorted with mock dismay. "When you start snoring, the bed does that much shaking it's like being in the middle of Hurricane Hilda."

Lucy laughed but in a moment she was thoughtful again. Tomorrow was a big day in their fight to have the pig's fields restored to him, for tomorrow would see the publication of the article about Ignatius in *The Kerry Sentinel*. She only hoped that the scatter-brained Travers would not let them down and then she set to work, helping her father to wash the dishes.

Chapter Eight

Early next morning, when Ignatius had completed both his aerobics routine and the briefest of stints on his exercise bike, both he and Lucy hurried down to the newsagency. The newspapers would surely have been delivered, Lucy assured the pig with rising excitement. Ignatius replied that he had no great confidence in that fellow Travers.

"You're out very early this fine morning," the friendly shopkeeper said when they entered the shop. "And how is Master Ignatius keeping, then?"

"Oh, he's fine. Fine!" Lucy replied hurriedly for this was not the moment to indulge in idle pitter-patter.

"I'll take a copy of *The Sentinel*, please."

The man took the price of the paper and placed it in the till, bidding her good morning as he handed the paper to her. Lucy had scarcely stepped into the street when she flicked eagerly through the pages – and she frowned with disappointment when her gaze fell upon the headline on page twelve.

"New Owner Has Big Plans For Ballymactaggle Hall"

And there beside it was a large photograph of the gentleman in question standing in dignified pose before the majestic doors of the great house. And where, Lucy wondered in dismay, was the photograph of the destitute pig, that had been abandoned by the world? The photograph that Travers had promised her would win a great deal of public support for their campaign.

Ignatius was somewhat relieved, however, that his own photograph had not appeared. It would have made him seem like some poor pig without a penny to his name when in reality he was a pig of means and was currently involved in the composition of his first musical.

"Listen to this!" Lucy said in frustration and she began to read aloud.

Mr Peregrine MacTaggle who has recently inherited MacTaggle Hall from his late grand uncle, has great plans to develop the property. One of his most ambitious projects is the establishment of a golf course on the estate which he says will attract many more tourists to Ballymactaggle.

"A golf course! Outrageous! Outrageous!" Master Ignatius exclaimed, forgetting that he was still on the street.

Ballymactaggle is an ideal location for a golf course, the new owner says, for not only is it within easy reach of Killarney it also boasts its own beautiful beach.

Lucy raised her eyes in despair. The report in the newspaper sounded like a party political broadcast on behalf of the golf club party.

Local businessman Tom Byrne will be Mr MacTaggle's partner in the golf club project and it is hoped to have the course fully operational by next year. This will involve the building of a clubhouse for members of the club which Mr MacTaggle hopes will be very select and exclusive. "No pigs allowed!" the owner of the Hall added wittily.

"Hubert always said Travers was a fool and how right he was!" the pig intervened. "A golf club!" he repeated with indignation. "Humans chasing little balls into little holes – and we pigs are accused of being unsettled!"

Lucy could hardly believe that Travers had given so much space to Peregrine and his plans for the Hall. There followed a glowing description of the house and the estate and the profile of the new owner as "both charming and refined". At last the disputed fields were given a brief mention:

"There has been some controversy about the ownership of the two fields on the estate but Mr Peregrine

describes the entire affair as no more than a storm in a teacup. The two fields in question are vital to the success of his golf club and he is totally opposed to the setting up of a donkey shelter. Such a centre would not only attract diseased, decrepit and unsightly animals to the area, animals which might stray hither and thither, but would also attract undesirables.

Lucy folded the paper gloomily. Travers hadn't even mentioned their petition and all the signatures they had collected in support of their campaign but what could they do now? The notion of a golf club on the estate was one that would surely appeal to a great many people in the village. It would give employment and attract tourists and Peregrine had cleverly conveyed the idea that the only obstacle in the way of his ambitious plans was the donkey shelter.

"Hubert had a dream, a dream of helping old, unwanted donkeys," Ignatius reminded her, "and we shan't give up without a fight. We'll have a meeting with Kelly at the Hall and we'll bring Gavin with us."

About two hours later Lucy, Ignatius, Gavin and the butler were seated about the fire in the cluttered Servants' Hall with its pannelled walls.

"Didn't I tell ye his lordship plied Travers with drink?" the old butler mused bitterly. "And he was charm itself, telling the fool he thought them that writes for newspapers leads very interesting lives."

Gavin looked downcast. Maybe he'd been clutching at straws but he'd been sure the donkey shelter would provide an answer to their prayers. If there was no donkey shelter then Fuchsia and Jasmine would have to return to the strand sooner or later and their fate would not be an enviable one.

"And didn't I know there was something goin' on when I seen Tom Byrne back and forth over these past few days," the butler went on. He glanced at a faded brown photograph in a silver gilt frame on the mantelpiece. It was a photograph of himself and

Mr Hubert that had been taken during one of the annual game shoots on the estate years and years before. Mr Hubert had been the last of the "rale oul' stock". "He'd turn in his grave if he knew that his grandnephew had it in his head to turn the estate into a playground for wealthy foreigners."

"If Master Ignatius don't stake his claim to his property soon he'll lose his rights entirely," the old man mused ruefully, "and 'tis thousands of pounds we'd want if we were thinkin' of goin' to court."

Master Ignatius had another idea, however, and now he shared it with his friends.

"We shall have a parade – a sort of protest march through the village down to the Hall," he explained. "One fears one has never been very keen on that sort of thing in the past – one has been something of a shy pig in that regard – though my cousin in Cork was a famous rebel. But now Peregrine has left us with no option!"

"A great idea," Gavin enthused.

"And this time we'll telephone every newspaper and every radio station in the country," Kelly said determinedly. "Golf club, indeed! 'Tis how I'd be afraid of my life to go for a stroll down the avenue for fear some fool would wallop my skull with a ball."

It was agreed that under no circumstances should they reveal their plans to Jarvis Travers.

"When will we hold the parade?" Lucy wondered, her ward again politely sipping a glass of white wine,

"As soon as possible, my dear," Ignatius replied when he had placed his glass aside. "Tom Byrne will soon begin to suspect foul play over the disappearance of his donkeys and we must have the entire matter sorted out by then."

"Saturday morning," Kelly said firmly. "That don't give us much time, today bein' Thursday. Lucy you'll see to the band, Gavin you can go round to ye'er friends and I'll make it my business to make a few phonecalls when his lordship is out."

"That's the spirit!" said Ignatius with some relish. "Onward! Onward! To the hour of glory!"

Lucy grinned at his passion. It was as if he could hear the roll of drums faintly in the distance. She said they would need posters too, but she and Gavin could take care of them.

"This could be our last chance at gettin' them fields for Master Ignatius," Kelly concluded, "so we'll have to pull out all the stops."

"It is gratifying to a pig in such circumstances as mine to know that he has friends who are good and true," said Ignatius, a tear trickling almost unnoticed from his right eye.

Lucy and Gavin spent much of the day recruiting members of the school band to join them in their parade on Saturday. The theme of the parade would be "Justice for Pigs!" and they would have a band practice in the community hall that evening after supper.

When they had had their lunch, Lucy and Gavin set about making posters for the parade. The kitchen table was cluttered with crayons and oil paints and watercolours but Gavin was very good at art. Lucy agreed with him when he said it was very important to have good posters – not just any old posters at all.

Soon his first poster was beginning to develop. It showed a little brown donkey like Fuchsia in front of a huge orange circle representing the sun. Above the picture was the simple message "Save the Donkeys" printed in bold black capitals.

"It's brilliant," Lucy said admiringly. She thought it was so brilliant, in fact, that she immediately decided to tear up her own first effort and cast it aside.

"Rachel's bound to hear about the parade," Gavin said anxiously. "She'll tell her father and he'll tell Peregrine."

"Just as well then – we told the others we were only going to march through the village," Lucy grinned, "just in case Peregrine decided to lock the avenue gates."

"Is your mother very disappointed that you're not moving house after all?" he asked, moving on to a different subject.

"She is a bit, but she's delighted with the piano," Lucy replied.

"Oh, can she play the piano?" Gavin asked, as he dabbed his

88

little paint brush into one of the oil paints beside him.

"No. No, she can't and neither can Dad and neither can I," his friend assured him good-humouredly, "but Mum wants me to learn and I'll give it a go for a while at least."

"I bet Rachel's green with envy. She's all the time boasting about all the things she has," Gavin replied. "I wouldn't be surprised if she makes her father get her a piano just to be as good as you!"

"I wonder how Jasmine and Fuchsia are getting on," Lucy mused. "Maybe they've had a drop of the poteen like the pigs."

Gavin grinned. "My uncle Matty pretends to be a crusty old guy," he replied, "but really he's cracked about animals. All his cows have names – not only names like Daisy and Bonny but grand names like Miss O'Rahilly and Miss Milligan."

Lucy smiled. He was probably referring to his new arrivals as Miss Fuchsia and Miss Jasmine.

At that very moment, Rachel was not very far away from the O'Brien household. She climbed furtively over the gate at the bottom of the back garden and skulked beside the wall of the shed. Lucy's mother had been boasting in the café about their new beautiful piano – the most beautiful piano she had ever seen – the shine from the wood had almost dazzled her eyes.

Of course, Rachel knew that Lucy's mother had been exaggerating as usual. The piano was probably some rickety old thing that was falling apart, from a retirement home for ageing woodworm. They had probably bought it at a secondhand junk shop and apart from the woodworm it was surely out of tune, too, Rachel assured herself spitefully. But then she had given in to an irresistible urge to go and see the piano for herself, which explained her presence in the O'Brien's garden in the late afternoon.

It would be such a laugh telling Mikey and the gang on the strand or in the chip shop about the O'Briens and their tumbledown wreck of a piano. Rachel stood and listened for a moment. The sweet tuneful tinkle of piano music came wafting towards her. Lucy O'Brien could never play as well as that. So who was in the shed? Rachel cast a wistful glance at the window set high in the old stone wall. If only she could reach it. There was something very mysterious going on and she was determined to get to the bottom of it. Then she thought of something. The Rooneys, a few doors down, had a stepladder and she could ask them for a loan of it for a few moments.

Rachel climbed over the gate once more, her heart drumming lest anyone should see her. Was it possible that Lucy's brother hadn't really gone to the Gaeltacht at all and that he was the one playing the piano now? Rory's mother had been singing the praises of the Irish college for months and if Rory had thrown a tantrum and decided not to go, Mrs O'Brien would surely be too embarrassed to tell everyone about it.

Maybe she had given him strict instructions to keep out of sight for a fortnight and perhaps he was banished to the shed for much of the day. That was surely it, Rachel told herself with glee, for now she would not only have the satisfaction of telling the world the truth about the O'Briens and their ramshackle piano. She would also have the added pleasure of exposing Rory's sham visit to the Gaeltacht.

"What is it you're wantin' the stepladder for?" Mrs Rooney asked suspiciously when she came to the door and found Rachel before her. Rachel was a great one for getting into trouble of one kind or another.

"Oh, it isn't for me. It's for Lucy O'Brien," Rachel lied with a charming smile. "Her little cat is after climbing a tree and he won't come down."

"I didn't know they had a cat at number 16," the woman retorted in the same suspicious tones as before.

"They haven't had it long – just a few days – it's a kitten really," Rachel explained as convincingly as possible, secretly wishing that the stupid old woman before her would give over her whinging and give her the ladder.

"Was it Lucy sent you down?" the woman asked, eyeing Rachel intently.

"Yeah, Lucy sent me and she told me to hurry because if she can't get the kitten down soon he's liable to fall and kill himself," Rachel lied again. Her tone was filled with such soft spoken concern that she might easily be mistaken for an angel with a heart of gold.

Mrs Rooney, though by no means as stupid as Rachel believed her to be, did eventually part with the much desired stepladder.

"And see you bring it back the minute you've finished with it, Miss," she called after Rachel, who thanked her heartily but who was soon secretly imitating her every word.

The stepladder was not very heavy and yet Rachel struggled with it as if it weighed a ton. When the girl reached the wall at the bottom of the O'Briens garden she paused to catch her breath and listen. It was just her luck if the mysterious musician had left his place at the piano. But just as she was about to plod back down the street in despair, the music came towards her once more and her expression brightened again.

She looked up and down the street – then with one determined heave she dumped the precious ladder over the wall. In a moment she herself was climbing over the forbidden gate. Lucy and Gavin were still too engrossed in their posters to be aware of the presence of the uninvited guest.

Rachel's heart began to pound with still greater force as she struggled to get the stepladder into position directly below the window, a window that had been set into the wall just below the roof. She didn't waste any time climbing the steps of the ladder and she grinned a mischievous grin as she imagined just how foolish the O'Briens would appear when she told her story to everyone. The glass on the window, however, was somewhat clouded and blotched and when she pressed her face against it, it took her eyes a moment or two to adjust to the blurred images beneath them in the shed.

The haunting rhythmic tinkle of the piano added to Rachel's feelings of suspense and tension. She squinted in an effort to see more clearly. Was she dreaming? Was she seeing things? Was there really a pig at the piano! Her dark eyes widened in dismay. It couldn't be a pig! Not the pig! She blinked and rubbed her eyes. It had to be an illusion, some trick of the light, and yet, there he was seated on the stool, a studious expression on his face as his foretrotters danced across the keys. Rachel was spellbound by the scene that greeted her eyes – the notion of a pig playing the piano was too strange, too crazy to be true.

It would be much better if she could convince herself that her eyes were deceiving her, but she could not do so, for the pig was at the piano and the pig was making music. These were the facts of the matter, the bald facts. A pig with Ignatius' pedigree might be expected to be a special sort of pig but who would believe her if she told them she'd seen a pig playing the piano. They would think she had a few screws loose but not only was the pig playing the piano and playing it very well, he was also pausing to jot down notes now and then.

Some moments later, Rachel reluctantly came down to earth once more. She tossed the stepladder over the wall and struggled over the gate. She was still in something of a daze as she laboured to return the ladder to the rightful owner.

"You look like you've seen a ghost, Rachel," said a man coming towards her with a dog.

"Maybe I have," the girl replied in a shaking voice but the man didn't understand.

Chapter Nine

Lucy and Gavin and their friends had a very successful band practice in the community hall that evening. Kelly the butler told them that he'd been speaking to someone in RTE and that their cameras would be in Ballymactaggle to cover the parade on Saturday. Rachel, however, was less than successful in convincing her long-legged friend, Mikey, that the pig could play the piano.

"Give over, Rachel," Mikey retorted with a grin when she told him the story in the chip shop, the twang of electric guitars screaming from the juke box. "Pull the other one!"

Nothing Rachel could say would persuade Mikey that she was telling the truth. Mikey still remembered the day she'd told him that the parish priest, who was cutting the lawn before the presbytery, was dressed in one of his housekeeper's frocks. And Mikey, like a fool, had believed her and had rushed up to the presbytery only to find that Father Nolan was looking for volunteers to sell tickets for some mission in Africa. Naturally, he had put Mikey down as his very first "volunteer".

Her father was even less sympathetic – advising her to act her age or people would think she was still in senior infants. Her mother only said, "Oh, really, a pig playing the piano, well, isn't that lovely!"

Rachel had always been such an imaginative child. And so it was with feelings of mild despair that Rachel made her way up to bed that night. She had to think of something to bring Miss Goody-Goody down a peg or two. The pig was the cause of all the trouble and it would be criminal if that pesky porker stood in the way of progress and prevented the development of the golf course.

Her father planned to sponsor competitions when the club was established and he intended donating a cup called "The Rachel Byrne Perpetual Trophy" for one of the ladies' competitions. "The Rachel Byrne Perpetual Trophy" – it had a nice ring to it but it might never come to pass if that pig put a trotter in the works. She had been so certain that her "Martha McFadden" act, when she had telephoned the Health Board, would surely mean curtains for the pig. The best thing that could happen would be for the pig to have an accident – no pig, no problem with the fields. But she was a bit squeamish when it came to blood – and black puddings turned her stomach. Maybe, just maybe, she could tempt Mikey to dispose of the pig for her. Maybe she could put out a contract on the pig and Mikey could play the part of the ruthless hit man, or in this case, hit pig.

She fell asleep and a strangely wonderful dream came to her. She stood in a flimsy black sequinned dress beneath a lamp post, her hair dyed blonde and bright pink lipstick on her lips. She was waiting for "him" – the soft yellow glow of the lamp light caressing her bare shoulders. She held a cigarette in a slim, black cigarette holder and took a drag now and then, exhaling wisps of smoke into the drowsy yellow night.

Soon she heard footsteps and her heart missed a beat. A dark figure came to her, dark hat, dark suit, dark glasses. He came and stood before her, smiling smugly as he placed his briefcase on the ground. He was chewing gum. He was always chewing gum.

"Got the dough, babe?" he asked, with a coolness that sent a delicious shiver down her spine.

"Yeah, I got the dough, Mikey, honey. Half now, half later," she retorted. "Ya gona fix that pig for me, ain't ya?"

"That pig is past tense, babe," the dark figure grinned as he placed the envelope that she handed to him in his pocket.

"Make sure ya do a good clean job, Mikser, no fuss, no mess, ya hear?"

"Yeah, yeah, sure thing, babe," was all he said. He reached down and took his briefcase in his hand. He released the lock and opened back the cover. He smiled a cold blooded smile as his fingers moved slowly across the contents of the briefcase. He turned the briefcase towards the lady in the sequinned dress and she gulped in dismay. There was nothing in the briefcase but a mirror and when she looked into the mirror she did not see her own image reflected there. Rather she saw the head of a pig attached to her body – a pig in a sequinned dress, a pig that looked so strange in a bright blonde wig.

"Come here, little piggy-wiggy. Come here, little piggy-wiggy," the dark figure resumed in tones that were hushed and menacing. He reached out to grab her but she fled in terror along the cobbled alleyway, struggling to keep her long black dress from trailing in the cobbled stones and stopping her progress.

"Come here, little piggy-wiggy," the words resounded through the empty blackness of the alleyway, for the lamp lights had all gone out. The dreadful echo of her own short spasmodic panting seemed to echo inside her brain. She came to a dead end. She groped the wall with her hand but there was no escape. She turned round to confront her aggressor but Mikey was now dressed in a white shirt, bow tie and black tuxedo and his hair, swept back from the forehead, was plastered with some kind of gel.

There was a silver piano with a candelabra and a vase of red roses on top. She moved towards the piano and began to play and Mikey began to sing in the most musical tones she had ever heard.

"My baby is a pig, I love her don't you see. My baby is a pig, she's the only pig for me. My baby is a pig, I love her night and day. My baby is a pig and a pig she'll always stay." And then he placed his microphone aside and took a saxophone in his hands. There came forth jazzy music that was mellow and soothing and oh, so laid back, but as he played his head, too, gradually became distorted and took on the aspect of a pig's head.

"My baby is a pig. Here eyes are so divine. My baby is a pig; I'm so glad this pig is mine." When they had finished the lights came up again and they found themselves on stage, their performance greeted by wild grunts of approval from the members of the audience who were all pigs, too. And who should pass by at that very moment but Lucy and Master Ignatius and they both carried golf clubs. To their utter dismay, Rachel and Mikey, still dressed in their formal evening wear, found themselves playing caddy for the girl and the pig. "Rotten luck,

Master Ignatius," Lucy said when the pig struck a ball that became wedged in the forked branches of a tree.

"Oh, I say, caddy," the pig called out, calling Rachel to him. "Be a dear, will you? Climb the tree and fetch my ball. We've decided to start the game again."

Rachel looked at the pig in his tweed cap, jersey and pants. She looked in horror at the height of the tree but in a moment she was climbing it as she'd been asked to do. Soon, however, the heel of one of her red stilettos became entangled in the hemline of her dress and she came tumbling down to earth. She seemed to fall down and down. The golfers and the greens and the bunkers were spinning round and round beneath her. It was a frightening sensation, for it seemed for a few moments as if she had flown free of her body but then, at last, she fell against the warm grasses. She felt cold, so cold, her pig face pale and tense as she lay outstretched before the assembled onlookers. Then one of the onlookers stepped forward and gallantly prepared to give her the kiss of life. She opened her eyes and the face of Ignatius swam before her. In a moment that face, smiling and kindly, was pressing down upon her...

She screamed and woke from her dream. It took Rachel a few moments to realise that all that had gone before had just been a dream and nothing more, but it made her even more determined than ever to outwit the pig and his mistress.

The next morning she stood daydreaming behind the counter of the café, the light of mischief shining in her eyes. A few moments later she raced upstairs and rummaged furiously in the drawers. She had been given a few posters by a passing circus troupe on the way to Tralee but she had kept one or two of them. There had been some information about forthcoming shows printed in small letters beneath the main section announcing the Ballymactaggle show. There had been a telephone number in Tralee where people could book in advance for the various performances. She just had to find those posters for without that telephone number she couldn't put her plan into action.

"What's gotten into you, this morning, girl?" her father snapped impatiently when he saw the scraps of paper and envelopes and invoices scattered all around. "I'm beginning to think you've flipped your lid. First you tell me the pig can play the piano and now you're pulling the place asunder like a raving lunatic – as if I hadn't enough trouble on my plate with not a trace of them blessed donkeys." He paused and buttered his toast. "If I find out someone's after whipping them from me, I'll skin them alive," he insisted in an angry voice. Then he sat deep in thought for a few moments, his expression dour and dark and menacing. He had never let anyone get the better of him and he'd be damned if he did so now. Suddenly he struck the table with his clenched fist, his face a mask of determination. Rachel eyed him nervously.

"By the way, I heard you scream during the night. What was that all about?" he demanded sternly.

"Just a bit of a nightmare – no big deal!" Rachel assured him as nonchalantly as she could, "but I'm looking for the circus posters. I thought I put one or two of them into a drawer somewhere."

"If you did, they must still be there for I've not seen them," the man with the flabby face assured her with the same disgruntlement as before. "What the devil do you want them for anyway?"

Rachel did not reply for a moment, her eyes brightening with delight when they came upon the much prized posters at last.

"Dad," she resumed vaguely, "don't you think it's good for people to travel and see new places?"

Her father looked at her suspiciously. She was up to one of her tricks again. He could feel it in his bones.

"Of course it's good to travel, girl," he assured her at length. "My years in England as a brickie made a man of me. Travel broadens the mind they say but it broadens the shoulders, too."

"That's what I think, too, Dad," Rachel grinned with satisfaction, "and wouldn't it be good if someone could help someone else to see more of the country?"

Another uneasy glance from her father.

"I haven't the foggiest notion what you're on about, girl," he told her sourly, "but I hope all this play-acting isn't just another excuse so's you can skive off from work again."

"I wouldn't dream of such a thing, Dad," Rachel said coyly and her father smirked.

Later, when Rachel found herself alone in the living-room she went to the telephone and dialled the number in Tralee that was printed on the poster. "Hello, this is Martha MacFadden from Ballymactaggle spaykin'," she began in her exaggerated rustic accent, when a soft-spoken voice answered the phone. " 'Tis to Mr Allgood, him who do own the circus, I'm wantin' to spayke to."

The soft-spoken voice was sorry to disappoint the caller but Mr Allgood wasn't available just then. It wasn't really his office, just a newsagency that handled the bookings for him whenever the circus came to Tralee. He usually called to the shop about ten-thirty, if Mrs MacFadden would like to call back then.

Mrs MacFadden very politely agreed to this and replaced the receiver. The minutes seemed to drag like hours as Rachel helped in the café kitchen but just before ten-thirty she found an excuse to go upstairs once more. "Mrs MacFadden" was in luck this time. Mr Allgood, the circus owner, was in the shop and was more than happy to take her call.

"The way 'tis with me, I have this little pet of a pigeen, sur," Mrs MacFadden began, "and the tricks he can do would put many's the Christian to shame. He do have that much sense he do think nothing of juggling and dancing – dancing, sur – and skipping the reel."

"He sounds like a remarkable pig, Mrs MacFadden," the circus owner observed, "but how, pray tell, may I be of assistance to you?" Mr Allgood's manner of expression was often as flamboyant as his clothes.

"Well, now, 'twas how I was thinkin', 'twas a shame to have the craythur hidden away from the public when he could make them all laugh till they were ready to cry," the "old lady" explained.

A pig that could make people laugh till they cried! This might be just the act he needed to add some more humour to the show, but he didn't wish to appear too eager.

"Pigs are not as popular as they used to be, kind lady," he assured the speaker at the other end of the line. "Time was when every household had a pig in the parlour; time was when a pig in the hand was worth two in the sty and a pig in time saved nine."

"But sure I would be lookin' for no great price for my pigeen," Mrs MacFadden assured him, "for 'twould be reward enough for me to think he was makin' a name for himself in the circus and 'twouldn't surprise me wan little bit if in years to come he wasn't the biggest pig in Irish showbusiness."

"Well, if that's the case I'll be more than happy to relieve you of your pig. Shall we say twenty pounds?" Mr Allgood suggested.

"Twenty pounds it is sur, oh, 'tis you are the dacent man, Lord bless you and keep you and may the road rise after you if not before you and if 'tis alright with your good self I'll have the pigeen in Tralee some time tomorrow evening after the dinner," Martha suggested.

More detailed arrangements were made and further pleasantries exchanged before Rachel replaced the receiver. A very satisfactory morning's work but still there was the small matter of capturing the pig and transporting him to Tralee. But, who better to help her than Mr Peregrine MacTaggle, who had, after all, the most to gain from the sudden departure of the pig. Indeed, one day Ignatius himself would surely thank her for as her father said "travel broadens the mind".

It was decided that Master Ignatius would assume the role of Grand Marshal and lead the parade, followed by Lucy, Gavin, Kelly and the school band. Their other schoolfriends and any other marchers who might decide to lend their support would follow. Master Ignatius put on a green necktie and sash and undertook what he called a trial run in the small pink living-room.

"Though I say so myself, I do cut rather a dashing figure, don't I?" the pig observed, turning about and studying his reflection in the mirror with immense pride.

"Oh, Ignatius, you look divine, a divine pig," Lucy's mother exclaimed in approval. "You're surely the finest pig that ever sported a sash in Ballymactaggle."

Ignatius took this compliment in the spirit in which it was intended though the thought did cross his mind that he was the *only* pig who had ever sported a sash in Ballymactaggle. Then he marched up and down in the limited space, which he had created in the middle of the room, his shoulders erect and his cane clenched stoutly between foretrotters. Lucy couldn't resist a grin. Ignatius was being adorably snooty again.

"One has always been proud of one's appearance," he continued. "There is nothing so despicable as a pig with sagging shoulder blades but sadly one sees them everywhere these days." He adjusted his necktie before the mirror above the fireplace. "The way one carries oneself speaks volumes about one's breeding, you know." He paused and studied his reflection more closely. "A rosette would not be suitable, I fear. Politicians wear them all the time and one draws the line at being associated with such company." He continued on in serious tones and Lucy grinned at the notion of a pig being mistaken for a politician or vice versa. She could just imagine Ignatius shaking hands – or trotters – with mothers and kissing their babies, a twinkle of glee in his eyes.

Lucy's mother made him some tea, her hand trembling visibly lest the precious cup should fall from her hand. Apart from the piano, Ignatius had ordered an entire china tea-set.

"I had all your fancy cups on the table when Tom Byrne's wife came by this morning – looking for information she was," the woman explained but the pig and the girl looked at her curiously.

"Well, the way she was hinting you'd swear we had the two donkeys hidden under the bed."

"Or maybe she fancied you had then concealed in your handbag," Ignatius replied with a touch of humour but Lucy looked anxious. It was plain that Byrne was suspicious that she and Ignatius and possibly Gavin, too, had been involved in the kidnapping of the donkeys. Her heart began to pound. Byrne simply couldn't find the donkeys before the parade the next day. If he did, it would ruin all their plans.

At that very moment the grumpy Tom Byrne was driving along the winding wooded roadway towards the old stonework farmhouse where Gavin's grand uncle lived alone. Jasmine and Fuchsia grazed happily in the field next to the farmhouse. That cheeky pup Gavin had made such a fuss about Jasmine's leg, Tom told himself shrewdly, that he might have been involved in the disappearance of the donkeys. And where better to bring them than to old Matty's farm?

Old Matty's brain was soaked with poteen and he was as mad as a hatter. These were the bitter thoughts that raced through Tom's mind as he swept along the winding country road. But no sooner had he rounded a bend than he was forced to brake suddenly, the car screeching to a halt. There on the grassy line that hugged the centre of the roadway sat the grey-haired, shaggy-bearded Matty, an old fishing hat flecked with flies set at a crazy tilt on his head. The old man appeared deep in thought, the kite he held in his right hand fluttering somewhat lazily in the dull skies overhead.

"Are you mad, man! I could've killed you!" Byrne screamed angrily as he leapt from his car.

"Whisht!" replied the other, with a gently dismissive wave of his left hand. "Can't you see I'm doing an experiment?"

"What bloody experiment?" Tom demanded.

"I'd be obliged to you, Mr Byrne, if you'd keep a civil tongue in your head," retorted the other as calmly as before. "If you must know I'm waiting to see how long 'twill take me to get airborne."

"Airborne?" Tom repeated in disbelief, arching his eyebrows in despair and looking at the bright red kite, brighter still against the deep grey fabric of the sky.

"It has always been an ambition of mine to fly," explained Matty with as much mischievous gravity and sincerity as he could fake, and when it came to faking he was the best. "When I come back the next time, I want to be a woodcock."

"Matty Sullivan, get off the road, you're drunk out of your skull," Byrne demanded with growing impatience, but Matty, keeping a firm grip on his kite, made no attempt to shift himself.

"Or if not a woodcock then at least a seagull," he persisted as if he'd scarcely heard the other's demand, "for a seagull is a great little fisherman and I've always had a *ghrá* for the fishing myself."

Tom moved to lift him forcibly from his place.

"Don't lay a hand on me Tom Byrne and I in the middle of my meditations and levitations and the devil knows what else," the other insisted more earnestly still. "I'd be halfway up the trees by now but for your ill-mannered outburst."

"I'm looking for my donkeys. Have you seen them?" Byrne demanded with rising frustration.

" 'Tisn't donkeys I have in my head at the minute. My thoughts is, as you might say, lodged on a higher plane," Matty retorted indignantly. He paused and rubbed his beard with his left hand, his mischievous blue eyes shining with glee. "And if all comes to all, can't I hire wan?"

"A donkey?" Tom replied in bewilderment.

"No, a plane, man. A plane. Sure donkeys don't fly," the other retorted with obvious impatience. "Though I'd prefer to leave the ground under my own steam. I'm on a diet, don't you see, to help what they calls my buoyancy."

"My donkeys! My donkeys!" Tom insisted, gritting his teeth in anger.

"Stewed cabbage and porter," the other persisted and again Byrne looked at him wonder, scarcely aware that he was now giving details of his new diet.

"My donkeys! My donkeys!" Tom screamed again, his face red and flushed with anger and disgust.

"A pheasant wouldn't be bad either," retorted the aged philosopher on the grass, rediscovering his old peace and mellowness all at once. He paused and eyed the other directly. "No, a pheasant wouldn't be bad at all if wan could be sure wan wouldn't get shot round the Christmas."

Byrne lifted his arms in despair and gnashed his teeth again. A few moments later he was backing his car into a nearby gateway and was driving furiously away. The old man remained as peaceful as ever, as if still thinking the deepest and most profound of thoughts. After quite some time, however, he rose to his feet, pulled in his kite, and stepped quickly up the road towards the field where Fuchsia and Jasmine grazed. He went into the farmhouse and brought them out some bread.

"Well now, my darlin' girls," said he, "what did ye make of my performance? 'Twas true for my nan when she said I missed my true vocation by not mounting the stage." Then he laughed heartily, and suddenly, impulsively the donkeys began to hee-haw too, as if they too enjoyed the trick he'd played on the tyrant Byrne.

Later that evening Lucy and her parents and the pig sat around the table in the kitchen at suppertime.

"I've been thinking about things," Lucy's mother began vaguely.

"What things?" her father asked.

"If my mother can learn to drive at her age, why can't I learn some new skill, too?" she replied.

"Like what?" Lucy wondered anxiously.

"Well, do you remember me telling you how I always wished I could do odd jobs around the house without waiting for someone else to do them?" her mother explained. Suddenly Lucy began to dread that her mother had dreamt up another hare-brained scheme now that the notion of moving house had been firmly knocked on the head.

"I've decided to take a DIY course – Do-It-Yourself – Mrs Rooney told me they're starting one in the technical school in September."

"God help me anyway," Lucy's father intervened with a good-humoured sigh. "A piano-playing pig and a DIY wife."

"I bet you think it's a good idea, don't you, Ignatius?" Lucy's mother went on turning to the pig for approval.

"A excellent idea, provided you do not propose to experiment in one's piano room," the pig answered pertly. But Lucy's mother was pleased with what she believed to be this very positive response.

"One is all in favour of accomplishments and refinements of one sort or another," Ignatius added helpfully.

Lucy grinned. The vision of her mother clattering away with a hammer and chisel could only very loosely be described as refined.

"Hubert was quite brilliant at the guitar until it took on the aspect of a Christmas goose – stripped bare from too much plucking."

Lucy looked at him quizzically – she did not understand.

"Plucked the strings once too often, my dear, and they simply fell asunder. He did make some homemade repairs with lengths of fishing line but it was never quite the same." He paused to sip his tea and take another slice of cake. "A guitar strung with fishing line is something less than elegant, I fear," he persisted gravely, "rather like a pig without a tail."

Lucy grinned, Master Ignatius turned towards her with an expression of the utmost seriousness.

"You may grin, my dear, but I have seen such creatures abroad in broad daylight. Have they no taste? No sense of what is required in polite society?"

Lucy grinned again. She couldn't help it. Master Ignatius was such an adorable little snob.

"I've made a start already. I've fixed that toaster I've been asking you to fix for ages, Joe," Lucy's mother announced triumphantly.

"Oh, have you now?" her husband answered with a look of disbelief that seemed to annoy his wife. She had seen that look before when Ignatius had suggested he might write his musical about pigs. Ignatius had proved him wrong and so would she, and so she rose suddenly from her place and removed the toaster from the cupboard. She placed it on the worktop, plugged it in and inserted two slices of bread.

"Now we'll see if you believe me," she said grimly as she

hovered beside the toaster like a protective mother bird fearful for the safety of her chicks.

"I think it might be time to take cover, Lucy," Joe O'Brien said in his good-humoured way as he pretended to find shelter beneath the table. Lucy laughed but she hoped that her mother's experiment would prove a success. A few moments later the two slices of toast were crisp, delicious and golden brown. The only trouble was that they took a notion to shoot through the air whereupon they entertained the company with a few fancy somersaults before coming to land once more – one on Lucy's lap, the other on top of Ignatius' head. Lucy's mother was not in the least discouraged, however. Nothing but a minor hiccup.

"Not a hiccup at all if your big into flying toast," Joe assured her.

Mrs O'Brien, however, insisted that she would pursue her DIY project to the bitter end. Master Ignatius looked suitably bewildered.

"One is keen on toast and marmalade for breakfast," he announced, carefully removing the toast, "but one rather draws the line at having it on one's head." Hereupon he made a mental note of the protective clothing he would need on further visits to the breakfast table – three layers, he judged, should be enough.

Lucy's mother would not be diverted from her idea to put up a shelf in the kitchen early next morning. She had a few old blue willow meat plates and they would make a nice display. Lucy was scarcely listening now, her mind firmly focused on the big parade next day. If the parade did not have the desired effect they could forget about the donkey shelter forever.

Chapter Ten

There was a buzz of excitement on the little streets of Ballymactaggle as the marchers assembled in the car park almost directly opposite the church. Kelly was smartly dressed in a white shirt and black suit with a red rose in his lapel. Ignatius looked positively radiant for he was wearing his best green necktie and sash, his attitude as always one of coolness and charm, His legal guardian, Lucy, was in a beautiful primrose dress, Gavin in a blue jumper and navy trousers, the members of the band in their deep green uniforms.

Lucy hugged Master Ignatius close to her for a moment before the parade began. She was hoping Peregrine might still see sense for it really wasn't a case of either a golf course or a donkey shelter as he had tried to suggest. If he surrendered the two fields which didn't belong to him he would still have plenty of land for his golf course.

Sunlight beamed down from a cloudless sky, Kelly looking earnestly at his watch now and then. The TV people had promised him they'd be on hand to capture the parade on film but now it was almost ten past ten and some of the marchers were beginning to feel a little restless.

Master Ignatius regarded being late as something akin to murder but now he held his peace though not without difficulty. Poor Hubert had always taken such a relaxed attitude to clocks. When it was seven o'clock in the hall it was merely five past four in the drawing-room, not to mention ten past eight on the landing. So many time zones in a single house! Though this did have certain advantages, for while one might be two hours late for tea, rushing through the hall, one found to one's utter delight one almost had an hour to spare when one finally reached the drawing-room.

They were just about to set off when who should appear on the scene but the smiling Rachel with one of her father's donkeys,

Whiskey Dew. Lucy looked at her with some apprehension. Rachel had been totally opposed to the idea of a shelter and this sudden conversion to the cause seemed more than a little suspicious. Rachel, however, played the part of the eager convert with conviction.

"My Dad didn't want me to come," she told Lucy with an innocent smile, "but I've been thinking about the poor little donkeys and I've decided it would be nice to try and do something for them."

Gavin was even more doubttful than Lucy.

"What game is she playing?" he whispered in furtive tones when Rachel and her companion moved away.

"Maybe she's really changed her mind," Lucy suggested, but it was an idea that did not even convince herself.

"I don't know," Gavin retorted warily.

"Seems to me like she's hatching some plot. I wouldn't be surprised if she wasn't just angling to get her face on tv," Lucy volunteered. That seemed a more likely explanation for Rachel's sudden change of heart.

Just as the parade was about to begin, the television crew arrived at last. They apologised profusely for the delay; they had had a puncture on the road to Killarney but they would like to get a few opening shots and maybe do a few interviews in the car park. The marchers looked on with rising interest as the cameras and lights were set up by the TV people. When the cameraman had filmed a few general shots, the reporter, a young woman in a check shirt and jeans, summoned Kelly and Gavin forward. She asked them to stand beside Lucy and Ignatius, who was hoping rather vainly that the camera would capture his best profile.

Of course, Rachel took it upon herself to move forward, too, so that she and Whiskey Dew could be seen clearly in the background. She imagined that viewers all around the country that evening would probably think to themselves, "What a sweet good natured child." The reporter had some questions to ask Lucy who explained again the terms of Hubert MacTaggle's will. She explained how Ignatius the pig, having inherited two fields wished to make his late master's dream of a donkey shelter a reality. Rachel would surely have seen fit to mimic Miss Goody-Goody's answers had she herself not been so clearly visible in the background. Instead, she smiled like a angel all the while, though she thought her face would crack for there was nothing so tough on the facial muscles as a smarmy insincere smile.

Kelly told the reporter how wonderful it would be if the shelter were set up, for he would love to see the little old donkeys of Ballymactaggle treated with kindness at the end of their days.

When the camera moved slightly to the left Rachel risked sticking out her tongue at Ignatius behind his back. She had never seen such a haughty pig in her life. But when she looked at his plump flabby legs she pictured him huffing and puffing as he struggled to skip through hoops in the circus. She could even hear the clicking of the whip as the trainer made him twirl massive balls on his snout. She sniggered to herself imagining his discomforture. Now that was a pleasing prospect if ever there was one.

She was more than a little annoyed, however, when the reporter didn't get around to interviewing herself. After all, she was the only one who had gone to the trouble of bringing along a donkey but she would have the last laugh and that was all that really mattered.

Very soon the marchers were stepping in sprightly fashion out of the car park, the rousing sound of tin whistles and flutes ringing in their ears, a fat little drummer boy beating the drum with considerable gusto. People gathered in doorways to watch Lucy and Ignatius lead the way, Gavin's beautiful poster of the donkey and the sun standing out amongst so many others that were proudly held aloft. The message on the poster "Save the Donkeys" was simple and sincere.

Though some of the donkeys of Ballymactaggle were old, they really were quite lovable, people said, and they deserved to be treated with dignity at the end of their lives. Although Ignatius was the subject of some very wry remarks it could not be denied that he was the legal owner of the fields.

"Do the pig think 'tis Patrick's Day or what that he's plastered in green?" asked an old woman of her companion, both of them laughing heartily.

"But he's a fine figure of a pig all the same, Hanny," retorted the other with the same good humour.

"Oh, aye, a darlin' to be sure, to be sure. Wan should love to take him home and have him for tea," replied the first.

"But wan do have to have the apple sauce for the roast pork."

The two of them laughed again. They were only joking, of course, for as Master Ignatius himself would have said he wouldn't be seen dead on a platter and apple sauce was hardly the thing when one's person was bathed in sandalwood. They paraded down through the village until they came to the great wrought iron gates of Ballymactaggle Hall. Here they paused for speeches on behalf of Ignatius, Kelly, Lucy and Gavin saying a few words in turn, their remarks greeted by loud cheering from their fellow marchers and Rachel cheered loudest of all. She glanced coyly at Ignatius now and then. If she had her way that pig would have volunteered to join the circus by nightfall.

Mr Peregrine was busy in the kitchen at the Hall. It would do his image no harm at all if he served the marchers some refreshments for they would surely make it their business to march up to the front of the house. Orange for the children, brandy for the cantankerous butler and a little white wine for the disagreeable pig. He fumbled in the pocket of his blazer and withdrew a sachet. When he had opened the sachet he poured the powder, a sleeping draught, into the glass of white wine that he would serve to the snooty pig. This would make the pesky porker more co-operative when they sought to whisk him off to Tralee. Then he hurried from the kitchen into the courtyard at the back of the great house.

The courtyard was enclosed by stables and outbuildings, many of them in a tumbledown state of repair. Hubert, for all his excellent qualities had never seen fit to trouble himself too much about such things.

"Hang it all!" he had been wont to say. "Holes in the roofs give the place a bit of character." He had been rather partial to ivies and mosses and lichens too and they grew rampantly all about the garden walls.

"Cut back a branch?" he was heard to exclaim with the greatest indignation one time. "Garden shears are the greatest menace since penny-farthing bikes." Then he had rambled on at length about how he had demolished a marvellous hydrangea when as a boy his penny-farthing had careered out of control and he had ended up amongst the leeks. "While one was uncommonly fond of leek soup," he had added, "sitting amongst them was never the thing."

Peregrine came to a locked garage and fumbled with the keys on the key-ring which he held in his hand. When he unlocked the door he reversed Hubert's battered old black car into the cobbled yard. Then he returned to the garage and took hold of a plastic gallon drum containing petrol with which he duly filled the petrol tank of the old black car. His grand uncle's car would be less conspicuous than his own top of the range white model when it came to transporting the pig to Tralee. "Transporting" – the word had a nice ring to it for it made it seem as if the innocent pig were in reality a villainous convict bound for some remote colony in Australia. It was a pity that the "cat-o-nine-tails" was not as popular as it had been in the old days for he would dearly enjoy the prospect of giving that porker a few hearty lashes.

Mr Peregrine had been told of the possibility that a TV crew might cover the parade. That was why he had secretly made arrangements for the refreshments and that was why he was determined to appear as charming as possible. He had also prepared a little speech, but he would, of course, give the impression that he was simply saying the first thing that came into his head.

Drugging a pig! The things he had to do to keep the estate

intact! A few moments later he was back indoors whereupon he set about taking the refreshments from the kitchen into the front hall. The girl and the butler had probably portrayed him as some hard-hearted pig-hating monster he assured himself grimly as he made his way through the corridors. But when the cameras rolled he would be all sweetness and light. He passed beneath a massive portrait of his grand uncle that hung in the passageway next to the front hall and he did not miss the opportunity to stick out his tongue and waggle it at the respectable old gentleman in the portrait. Stupid old buzzard! If it hadn't been for him he would not have to resort to plotting foul play on a pig.

The songs of birds cascaded through the trees as the marchers made their way along the avenue.

"I never thought I'd see the day when I'd be taking a stand against wan of the MacTaggles," Kelly the butler mused in regretful tones. "Mr Hubert, Lord rest him, did right by the people."

"Maybe Peregrine will change his mind about the fields when he sees all the bad publicity he's getting," Lucy speculated, more in hope than in confidence.

"I just hope he don't turn the whole show on its head like he did with that fool, Travers," Kelly retorted grimly.

Kelly's fears were well founded for as soon as the parade came within view of the imposing walls of the great house, the dapper Mr Peregrine emerged, smiling a kindly smile. He smiled and he smiled and he smiled like some bountiful lord and master of the manor, ready to welcome the peasants with open arms – to listen with seeming interest to their little humdrum problems, then ply them with sweet and winning words, toss them a few crumbs from his table and send them on their merry way once more, all happy and cheerful and bright.

"So nice to welcome you all to the Hall," he began in his charming way when the parade finally came to a halt. "I think I know the reason for your visit but I feel honoured, very honoured that you chose to come to share your views with me personally."

Kelly wrinkled his forehead. There was no denying it but

111

Peregrine was a great wan for the *plamás*. 'Twas no wonder Travers had fallen for it hook, line and sinker.

"I'm sure that the walls of this great and noble house have seen many festive occasions down through the years and though there may be differences between us, this gathering today is also a festive occasion of sorts."

"Festive occasion!" Ignatius muttered sourly to himself. "Peregrine MacTaggle, you look more like Scrooge than Father Christmas, you infernal windbag!"

"That is why I invite you all to partake of a little light refreshment before we begin our discussions," Peregrine went on with the same attitude as before.

Soon everyone was sipping merrily and what had begun as a protest took on the aspect of a picnic.

"We'd like you to tell us if you intend returning Master Ignatius' fields to him or not," Kelly asked bluntly, determined not to allow matters to drift any further.

"I'm afraid I can't give you a direct answer on that one," the ever-charming Peregrine replied. "My solicitor handles all my business for me but I would be happy to have a private little chat with the pig and his legal guardian to see if we might not come to some agreement."

About ten minutes later Ignatius complained of dizziness and Mr Peregrine kindly invited him to come inside and rest.

"Are you alright, Ignatius?" Lucy asked anxiously. "I hope you haven't been too excited about the parade and everything."

"I'm feeling rather queasy, my dear," the pig confided glumly, staggering ever so slightly but as always it was a very elegant little stagger.

Soon, however, he began to feel like those common swine at old Matty's farmhouse must have felt when they had come upon them lurching all over the road.

"One rather fears it seems as if one is intoxicated," the pig persisted in bewildered tones. "Such an indignity and on such a very public occasion, too."

Now Jarvis Travers appeared on the scene and began to wield his camera with great relish. Lucy scowled at him darkly for she could just imagine the headlines in his rag of a newspaper. "Pig Turns Parade into Drunken Spree!" or "Stately Pig in Swinish Scramble!"

"Stuff your camera up your gansey," Kelly demanded. Travers chuckled foolishly to himself, for here was another glorious opportunity for a riveting headline "Grumpy Butler Acts the Goat" or "Butler Threatens Violence".

"I'm afraid I must have a lie down, my dear," said Ignatius abruptly, now looking positively withered about the snout.

"I'm coming with you to make sure you're alright," Lucy insisted.

"No, no, you can't. You must go back to the village with the parade. There may be other reporters," Ignatius protested. He paused and added gravely. "When the general is wounded, his troops soldier bravely on. Besides, Kelly can stay with me."

And so it was that the old loyal butler led his late master's favourite porker beyond the hallowed doors of the Hall once more. Kelly was more than a little surprised when the new owner of the Hall suggested they might use the old plum-coloured drawing-room. Ignatius heaved a sigh of regret when he saw the old room again and the memories came flooding back.

He struggled onto one of the easy chairs beside the fire, the butler urging him to rest and take things easy. The past few days had been fairly hectic, the kind of days that would put a strain on the best of pigs, even pigs of noble descent. It was with great reluctance that Lucy had yielded to her aristocratic ward's plea that she return with the parade to the village. After all, she was the pig's legal guardian and if anything happened to him she would never forgive herself. He assured her that he would be perfectly safe as long as Kelly remained close to him.

Kelly remained close to Ignatius for quite some time but when the pig fell asleep he decided to make his way to the kitchen to prepare a little wine and strawberry cocktail which would surely be to the patient's liking when he woke once more. The moment the butler took his leave of the drawing-room, however, Peregrine and Rachel pushed open the door and they smiled with satisfaction when they saw the sleeping beauty on the chair.

"What a happy little pig!" Peregrine gloated as he and his accomplice drew near to their victim with a large rectangular rushwork laundry basket. They were like merciless hawks preparing to pounce on a defenceless chick. Peregrine took hold of Ignatius' head and Rachel grabbed hold of his rear and then they struggled to lift the sleeping porker into the basket. They struggled and they struggled, panting and puffing, for Master Ignatius was, as he admitted himself, a little plump.

Rachel's imagination began to run wild again. She and her accomplice Peregrine were special agents sent on a daring mission to rescue the Prince of the House of Pigs and to carry him safely back to his own country, Pigsylvania. The royal prince was but a babe in arms – a bonham in arms to be more precise. That was why the government, acting on behalf of the royal family, had chosen two of its most brilliant agents to effect the rescue. That was why she and her partner had risked life and limb to ensure that his Royal Pigginess took his rightful place on the throne. There was indeed every possibility that the handsome and precious prince would one day marry the beautiful heroine who had saved his life and she would have the honour to become the Queen of the Pigs. That was a dream to cherish but just as she began to hear a flourish of trumpets, just as she began to picture the royal wedding she was rudely awakened.

"Stop dawdling, girl, and get the pig into the basket – this was your idea, after all," Peregrine insisted with increasing urgency.

Again the conspirators huffed and puffed like the big bad wolves of long ago until at long last the precious pig was dumped unceremoniously into the laundry basket, whereupon Mr Peregrine covered him with sheets. He then hurried away for a moment, telling Rachel it would be necessary for him to lock the butler in the kitchen or in the Servants' Hall. They didn't want anyone raising the alarm until it was much too late.

Chapter Eleven

The seconds seemed to drag like hours as Rachel waited for her accomplice to return and she fixed her gaze on the porcelain mantle clock. She watched the second hand move slowly, relentlessly forwards. She heard footsteps in the hall and in a moment Peregrine was beside her once more. He had taken care of the butler and the car was at the front door.

"I didn't know pigs were so heavy," Rachel grumbled as they struggled to carry the pig to the car.

"Stop moaning girl and get on with it," her accomplice snapped. "Do you know what we could get for pignapping?"

"No, as a matter of fact, I don't know what we could get," the girl retorted with a cheeky smirk.

"Neither do I and it's best we don't find out," Peregrine replied, his charm having suddenly deserted him.

When the pig in the basket was safely ensconced on the back seat of the car, Peregrine switched on the ignition and drove swiftly out of the estate by a side route. This allowed him to bypass the village entirely. What would she tell Mr Allgood, Peregrine asked as he grinned with satisfaction. She would tell him she was Martha MacFadden's grand-daughter. Her grandmother couldn't come because she had come down with a dose of popolopolitis – and with any luck it might prove terminal. Peregrine was beginning to feel a little more relaxed and he laughed heartily. The girl was hilarious.

At that moment, however, Kelly the butler was rummaging furiously through the old writing desk in the Servants' Hall in search of a key. When he found it he hurried to the telephone and rang the café, telling Lucy's father that Ignatius had disappeared and that he suspected foul play. Joe O'Brien collected his daughter at the car park and seconds later they were on their way in his car.

"I knew Rachel was being too nice! I knew it!" Lucy said, her face a mask of apprehension. Kelly had seen Peregrine drive old

MacTaggle's black car past the pantry window and if he had directed his course towards Killarney he would have had to drive past the marchers. It therefore seemed logical to conclude that he was heading for Tralee.

"There's a bacon factory in Tralee!" Lucy exclaimed in horror. "You don't... you don't think he's bringing Ignatius there?"

"Could be!" her father replied frankly as he pressed his foot more firmly on the pedal, the speedometer revealing that the deep green Opel Cadet was now travelling at almost sixty miles an hour. "It isn't exactly a major crime to kill a pig."

"But he's not Peregrine's pig," Lucy insisted.

"I know that and even if Peregrine's plotting some terrible deed, we may be able to overtake him," her father answered more reassuringly.

Meanwhile, Mr Hubert's old black car swept along at a furious pace along the mountain road to Tralee but it seemed to Rachel as if they weren't moving at all. It seemed as if it were the fields bearded with coarse green grasses that went whizzing by.

There was some movement in the basket as Ignatius struggled to rouse himself from his sleep. Where on earth was he? It took him a few moments to appreciate that he had taken up residence in his late master's laundry basket and that he was being taken for a ride by the new master at the Hall. How dare the fellow confine him to a laundry basket like some tattered old dishcloth! Most unbecoming – to have one's dignity reduced to that of a soiled napkin, to have one's person take on the character of a crumpled bedcover. He would not stand for it! He would not stand for it!

"It's the pig, he's shuffling about," Rachel told the driver.

"No need to worry – the catch on the basket is quite secure," Peregrine assured her.

"I can't wait to see Lucy O'Brien's face when she finds out that her stupid pig has done a vanishing act," Rachel smiled with anticipation. The pig in question was now butting the cover of the basket with the top of his aristocratic head. Rachel wondered if she should open the basket.

"Mr Allgood would not be too impressed," she said, "if the porker had a lump on his noggin." Peregrine did not object for the pig might be suffering from claustrophobia and after all he couldn't possibly escape. Master Ignatius fumed with indignation but he maintained an obstinate silence at least for the time being. It was just when Rachel had lifted the cover; just when Ignatius had popped a very disgruntled head out of the basket that the O'Brien's car came into view a little distance behind them.

"Look! Look! It's them!" Lucy cried. "And there's Master Ignatius!"

"Don't worry, they won't get away from us now," Joe O'Brien told his daughter. It was with some difficulty that he concealed a grin for he had heard of people trying to kidnap racehorses and royalty but never pigs.

"Step on it!" Rachel screamed at Peregrine as the O' Brien's car drew nearer and nearer but Peregrine retorted saucily that if he stepped on it anymore his leg would go through the floor. Rachel turned to glance at the chasing car again and again, her heart pounding as it had never done before. She would never live it down if she were outsmarted by little Miss Goody-Goody.

Next moment, Peregrine's fears about the road worthiness of his uncle's car became a reality when the gear stick came away in his hand! His eyes widened in dismay but worse was still to come for when he pressed on the brake pedal as he approached a sharp bend he found to his horror that the brakes were not working.

"We're going to be killed!" Rachel screamed when her companion shared the bad news with her.

"Damn and damn again!" Peregrine retorted in frustration, beads of sweat beginning to glisten on his forehead. "Damn me for being so stupid for I should have guessed from the state of the house that my pig-headed grand uncle wouldn't spend a penny on maintaining his car."

"What do we do now?" Rachel asked, covering her eyes, afraid to look at the road before her. She was sure that some cow or bullock or heifer would wander out of some farmyard or laneway at any moment now.

It was at this moment her heart missed another beat when Ignatius curtly expressed a view that it served them both right!

"The pig – the pig, he can talk!" Rachel gasped at the forlorn Peregrine who was still awkwardly clutching a piece of the gear stick in his left hand. He simply replied that nothing would surprise him now.

"If you will kindly move aside, sir, I shall take charge of the situation," the pig snapped, once again assuming the tone and attitude of an angry general. In a moment Ignatius was scrambling precariously out of the basket and was struggling onto the front passenger seat beside the wide-eyed Rachel. Then he grabbed hold of the steering wheel with his two front trotters and manoeuvred himself onto the driver's seat while the bewildered Peregrine manoeuvred himself in the other direction. In a moment the pig was at the wheel, his two companions cramped together on the passenger seat.

Lucy looked at her father in dismay. Ignatius had now taken over the driving of the car in front of them, so why didn't he slow down and stop?

"Looks like he's having a problem with the brakes," her father answered and a shiver tingled down Lucy's spine.

While Rachel and Peregrine cowered in a huddle the pig told them that this was what came of bad strategy.

"If one takes the trouble to plan a mission, a raid or anything of that nature," he insisted, "one should not approach it as if one were making a pancake – half in the frying pan, half in the air!"

Peregrine's eyes grew wider and wider. He had always thought his uncle was stone mad but now he was beginning to see that the old man had not been so daft after all.

"Mr Hubert used to say his brake pedal was always a bit temperamental," the pig went on haughtily. "It's just a case of being firm with it."

However old, the old black car swept through the town of

Tralee, shooting through traffic lights as if they were mere figments of the imagination and swerving this way and that to avoid the oncoming traffic.

"Be the holy, is it a pig is driving that vehicle?" asked an old woman on the pavement. "I thought people only dressed up for the biddy and the wren."

" 'Tis likely some kind of publicity stunt," her companion answered knowingly. "Keep your eyes open – look out for any cameras."

Rachel thought her end was nigh when a big Guinness lorry came chugging towards them. But Ignatius swung sharply to the left, grazing the side of a blue Toyota that was just about to move away. Was it any wonder that the driver of the Toyota assured herself angrily that some male drivers could be real pigs.

It was only a matter of time before the porker's reckless driving came to the notice of a vigilant garda on a motorcycle. Soon he was in hot pursuit, the car cruising along Rock Street and sending other vehicles scurrying this way and that like so many clucking hens. Bitter words were spoken and fists were raised in anger as cars bumped into cars or had close encounters with lamp posts and poles and litter bins. Still the old black car moved resolutely forward, its occupants apparently oblivious to all the mayhem and havoc they were leaving in their wake.

Master Ignatius was now, however, doing a little fancy footwork on the brake pedal. Whenever Hubert had wanted to bring the car to a halt he had tapped his foot to the rhythm of some old marching tune – brake pedals were suckers for marching tunes he used to say. It was bad enough having a pig as a driver but a crazy pig was ten times more lethal entirely, Rachel thought. Did he really expect the car to stop by doing a pig and whistle version of the highland fling on the brake pedal. But Peregrine snapped at her to hold her tongue unless she had a better idea. Ignatius leered disdainfully as if her contribution were beneath contempt. The way they were going it wouldn't surprise him if they had completed the circuit of Ireland by nightfall, Peregrine said.

Despite these less than encouraging remarks, the pig patiently persisted with his tapping routine. At last his efforts were rewarded when the car shuddered uneasily to a halt. His two passengers heaved a sigh of relief but Ignatius promptly clambered onto the top of the seat. He then made an athletic leap, that would have done any circus master proud, back to the basket once more.

When the garda came to the window a few seconds later, he stared blankly at the empty driver's seat and demanded to know if Peregrine had been driving the vehicle. The pig had taken the further precaution of draping himself with the sheet in the linen basket.

"No, I w..wasn't driving the vehicle," Peregrine answered with a dazed stammer. " I mean, I was driving at first but then... "

"But then... ?" the garda prompted." 'Tis how you'll be trying to persuade me 'twas the pigeen there was doing the drivin'."

"Well to be perfectly frank, my good man, the pig *was* driving the vehicle," Pergrine insisted with great indignation.

"Do you tell me now?" Garda Murphy retorted wryly. "Well, if that's the case, 'tis how I'll have to be askin' you to follow me back to the station where you'll not mind blowin' into a little bageen for me, for 'tis thinkin' I am you've had wan too many."

"Now look here, officer, I say, I'm not in the least intoxicated, really I'm not," Peregrine insisted again.

"No, no, of course, you're not, sir," the garda grinned, "and the judge would be thinkin' I was a sound bloody man if I hauled a pig before him for dangerous drivin'."

Peregrine was about to protest again but Garda Murphy told him that if he didn't shift himself out of the car "at once", he'd have to charge him with another offence, that of resisting arrest.

MacTaggles's grandnephew glared at Rachel as he moved across to the driver's seat. It had all been her fault. If she hadn't proposed that absurd notion of selling the pig to the circus none of this would have happened. Rachel, however, was still visibly shaken when Lucy came rushing up the old black car.

She jumped for joy when Ignatius peered nonchalantly at her

from the basket. She might have been angry at Rachel were it not for the fact that Rachel was still recovering from her hair-raising experience. After all, the prospect of being squashed like a sardine in a tin beneath a Guinness lorry hadn't exactly made her day. Lucy opened the car door and the pig leapt out with a great deal of coolness and style from his place of confinement. Lucy's father smiled at his daughter when she hugged and cuddled the pig as if he were some porcine teddy bear.

"Poor, poor Ignatius, are you alright?" Lucy asked with undiminished intensity.

"Perfectly fine, my dear," he insisted dismissively. "It was all rather exciting in the end, you know. One does not wish to appear boastful but one always suspected one was made of the stuff of heroes."

Lucy grinned. Already she could hear the national anthem being played in the background and there was some crusty old sergeant-major pinning a medal on the pig's lapel. The gallant Ignatius, shoulders erect, his gleeful little eyes shining with something less than humility. Lucy grinned. She was relieved to see that despite his ordeal her friend had lost none of his endearing self-importance and that was a good sign, a very good sign indeed.

Joe O'Brien had a few harsh words to say to Mr Peregrine, however. If Mr Peregrine didn't reconsider his decision about the disputed fields, he could add a third charge to his list – that of falsely imprisoning and abducting a pig. Mr Peregrine tried to appear calm but deep down he was quaking with fright – dangerous driving! Resisting arrest! Abducting a pig!

If that sort of thing got into the social columns of the newspapers he might as well emigrate to outer Katmandu. "There had been a most regrettable misunderstanding," he assured Lucy's father.

Solicitors could be incredibly stupid at times but he would see to it personally that Master Ignatius' fields were restored to him as a matter of urgency. And he would have no objections to the donkey shelter, Lucy's father persisted. Lucy grinned from ear to ear like a cat that had just staggered into a plate of cream. No, no, he would have no objections to the donkey shelter, Peregrine stammered as if the words were almost choking him. The fields were fairly secluded by trees and so the donkey shelter would hopefully not interfere with his golf course – the plans of which would have to be slightly modified.

Lucy could scarcely believe her ears but it seemed that at last Master Ignatius was to have his property returned to him. Rachel looked glum. Who would have thought that the dumb pig could not only talk but could also drive a car? Of course, these were stories she would not be sharing with the boys in the chip shop. Mikey and the others were already beginning to think that she might be a bit crazy but she didn't blame them. How were they to know that for once she wasn't messing – that the pig really could play the piano.

Garda Murphy still insisted that Peregrine should accompany him to the Garda Station but Joe O'Brien asked the Garda to go easy on him. He explained that Peregrine had had a bereavement in the family in the recent past and that, he suggested, might have caused him "to lose the run of himself for an hour or two." That would be taken into account, the garda assured the girl's father.

Some time later Lucy and her father, Ignatius and Rachel, returned to Ballymactaggle, the marchers, singing and dancing for joy when they heard the good news. Lucy and Gavin must make the necessary arrangements for the donkey shelter, Ignatius told his legal guardian when they sat at the supper table that evening. He himself would be far too busy with his pig's musical and he was thinking of taking up tennis. His early morning exertions in front of the television were making him feel like a bit of a ham – rather unbecoming for a pig of quality. As for his exercise bike, it was quite the worst investment he had ever made. Anyone could see it was defective in almost every detail. Tennis, now that was a game beyond the compass of ordinary swine. Lucy grinned.

"But what about your mint humbugs?" she wondered mischievously.

"Oh, one must have one's mint humbugs, my dear," the pig told her with the utmost gravity. "The latest medical research, I believe, is that they are not at all as fattening as they were once thought to be."

"Medical research! The pig would be going about with a stethoscope one day soon," Joe O'Brien told himself merrily. Ignatius paused to sample a piece of chocolate cake as he sipped from his china tea cup.

"One simply must keep abreast of the latest medical opinion if one is to follow a sensible diet. To be perfectly frank, my dear, one had always rather suspected that mint humbugs were quite an aid to one's stamina. After all, one feels positively energetic when one has had four or five."

"Tennis and musicals and medical research!" Lucy's father sighed – the pig was losing the run of himself again, suffering from delusions of grandeur. Of course, Lucy's mother thought the tennis was a great idea and she would like to have a go at it, too. She had been a great fan of Wimbledon for years, even when it rained.

"Great fan of Wimbledon!" Joe O'Brien rolled his eyes. The woman knew as much about tennis as she did about DIY and she had, it seemed, spent her day hacking big chunks out of the wall to put up a shelf for her much-prized plates. The shelf had such an incredible slant it would make him seasick if he had to look at it for long, he assured himself. Lucy's mother, however, was very proud of her work. It was quite amazing but if one tilted one's head slightly to the right, the shelf appeared perfectly straight. Her husband could just imagine their visitors being encouraged to tilt their heads to admire the straightness of the shelf.

"It's not a bad effort, not a bad effort at all," he said when asked his opinion of the shelf, "and as you say, you'll probably do better when you start your DIY class."

Lily O'Brien smiled contentedly. She knew she had done a good day's work but it was nice to hear Joe talk so approvingly of her shelf. Poor Dad, Lucy mused to herself. He never kicked up a fuss about any of her mother's schemes – moving in to live with their grandmother, getting a piano for Ignatius, even taking on a perilous pastime such as DIY. Who could tell what might lie in store when her mother really got going with the hammer and chisel? "Love is a quare thing," Kelly the butler sometimes said. Love could be the only explanation for her father and mother getting on so well together.

Later Lucy was in pensive mood as she sat in the music room that in a former life had been the "multi-purpose outbuilding of some character," the pig tinkling away at the piano. Kelly and Gavin, Nick and Matty had all been so happy when she had told them that Peregrine had decided to return the fields to Ignatius after all.

Fuchsia and Jasmine's future was assured. Mr Philbin the solicitor was negotiating to buy the two of them on his client's behalf. Lucy tried hard to imagine what things would be like in a few years' time. It would be hard work but the shelter would be built and six or seven donkeys would have found a happy home, grazing peacefully during the day time and snoozing snugly during the night. In her mind's eye she saw a sign at the newly constructed gateway. A sign which not only bore the words, "Asaleen Donkey Shelter" but which was also embellished with the image of the donkey and the sun which had appeared on Gavin's beautiful poster.

And what of Ignatius? What would he have achieved in a few year's time? She looked at him now as he sat and played and sucked a mint humbug. He would have attended as the guest of honour at the gala premier of his hit musical "The Adventures of a Prodigious Pig". His ability to speak would no longer be a relative secret and he would have appeared on several TV chat shows in Ireland.

Lucy imagined him sitting in relaxed mood in an armchair and discussing his musical achievements with great enthusiasm. He would probably have been elected Honorary President of the Ballymactaggle Tennis Club, a club established by himself. The ladies' captain, if such were allowed in tennis clubs, being Lucy's mother who would also have been awarded the prestigious International Award for Ingenious Shelf Construction, a trophy proudly but precariously displayed on the first and most historic of these shelves in the kitchen.

Lucy turned towards Ignatius again and smiled with satisfaction. He was the most wonderful friend in the world. It was no idle boast, she said, to suggest that he was the most unprecedented, unparalleled pig in the glorious history of Ballymactaggle swine. The day would surely dawn when the citizens would raise a statue in his honour – and on the bottom of the statue would be a plaque bearing the simple but moving tribute: "Ignatius MacTaggle, the Uncrowned Pig of Ireland."

"Too kind, my dear, too kind," said Master Ignatius, his foretrotters sweeping nimbly across the shining keys. Then he paused and offered her a mint humbug which she gladly accepted. "Such a relief not to have to be deprived of one's humbugs," he added seriously and Lucy could not a resist a smile.

Watch out for some other great books from
BLACKWATER PRESS

The Cally

by Turlough McKevitt

Following a walk on Slieve Gullion, a strange creature stalks John Kett. Curious things begin to happen. Rex the dog mews, the Ketts fly and Mary Kett almost jumps out of a giant nut!

Granny clashes with Olivia Jolson, the famous theatrical director, during the staging of the pageant to celebrate the finding of the "Gretel Stones".

Meanwhile... events draw them all towards the Mountains of the Hag, where they are eagerly awaited by... **THE CALLY.**

The Yuckee Prince

by Larry O'Loughlin

When Witch Wendy Way is asked to babysit Prince Alysious Tripod Jefficus, she can't believe her luck. After all, it has only been two days since she left the Grimwood Academy for the Training of Wizards and Witches.

But she soon finds out that *luck* isn't always *good* luck, when the sweet little prince with the face of an angel lives up to his well-deserved nickname of *"The Yuckee Prince"*.

Reaching The Heights

by Peter Gunning

Tosh and Naylor live in the notorious "McGillicuddy Heights" where growing up fast is a necessity for survival. Their schoolfriend Aisling is from the more fashionable side of town but when her family begins to split up, Aisling too must develop survival techniques of her own.

When Naylor vows to discover the identity of his mother's attacker Tosh and Aisling agree to help.

Reaching the Heights is a fast-moving story of how the three young teenagers tackle all obstacles with courage, ingenuity and humour.